RUTHIE

ANGIE GIBSON

Twisted Dreams Press

Cover image by: Angie Gibson

Layout and Design by: Jennifer Horgan

Edited by: Jennifer Horgan

Twisted Dreams Press

twisteddreamspress.com

To Ted Watts:

You left us too soon but you are always in my heart.

"When I'm losing my control, the city spins around You're the only one who knows, you slow it down" –The Fray

TABLE OF CONTENTS

CHAPTER ONE

Ruth Ann Hamilton, known as Ruthie, was just six years old when she vanished from her small town of Lakeview, GA, a community of roughly 5,000 residents. Her disappearance sent shockwaves through the town, instilling a fear among parents that they had never known before. How could a child simply disappear from their seemingly safe town?

In the midst of this crisis, Ruthie's mother and stepfather were tirelessly reaching out to the media, desperately seeking any leads or information. The sense of urgency and despair was palpable, not only for her family but for the entire town. The police launched a comprehensive search effort, deploying search dogs, teams, and helicopters in their quest to find her. Even Ruthie's biological father, who had been absent from her life since before her birth and lived on the opposite coast, was questioned as part of the investigation.

Dylan, Jalen, Dakota, and Pedro knew a kid had disappeared and that her parents were upset. They knew they couldn't stay out after dark any longer and could hardly escape their parents' watchful eyes to go to their clubhouse in the woods. They understood, but only as much as 12-year-old kids can understand. Basically just enough to know something scary had happened, and they couldn't play like they normally did. Three days after she went missing, school was out. The school year ended, and summer began. The boys were home and bored. It was the presence of bored 12-year-olds in their houses, aggravating their parents and siblings, that finally caused their parents to relent enough to let them go to the playground where all the parents in their neighborhood were taking turns keeping an eye on the kids. With that many kids running around, it made it easier for them to slip off into the woods to their clubhouse.

"Did anyone see you?"

Dylan's voice echoed with a mix of excitement and urgency as he glanced around, catching his friends' eyes. The treehouse loomed above them, nestled securely among the sturdy branches of a towering oak. It perched about 15 feet off the ground, a modest yet welcoming fortress constructed by Dylan's older brother last summer. Its wooden exterior, weathered and rugged, spoke of countless adventures and lazy afternoons.

The interior was a cozy patchwork of practicality and imagination. A wooden bench, seamlessly wrapped around the trunk of the tree, created a circle of seating that invited endless conversations and games. Along one wall, a set of simple cabinets offered a makeshift storage solution, holding everything from forgotten treasures to emergency snacks. The rest of the space was an open expanse, where old sleeping bags were spread out like colorful rugs, and crates served as makeshift tables, their surfaces cluttered with a mix of board games and comic books.

The treehouse was more than just a structure; it was a retreat from the ordinary, a place where the outside world was momentarily forgotten, and only the camaraderie of friends and the thrill of youthful escapades mattered.

"Nope!" they replied in unison.

Dylan pulled out a newspaper he'd picked up from a bench, and the boys began pouring over it. So far, their parents had tried to keep them away from the TV and papers, even the Internet, to try and protect them from the fear that they themselves felt so keenly. But the boys had been listening anyway and sneaking looks on the computer while playing their video games to try and get some information. Not to mention, they all had cell phones.

"Do you think she just ran away?" Pedro asked.

"No way. They would have found her by now. Where could she go around here?" Jalen shot back. "She's been snatched by some perv or something for sure."

"You don't know that," Pedro said, frowning. Jalen had lived in a bigger city up until a year ago and touted himself the more "worldly" of his group of friends.

"Man, I'm telling you. Some creepy perv snatched her, and she's gone for good," Jalen replied, shoving the newspaper at Pedro. "See!"

The paper's headline read:

KIDNAPPING SUSPECTED IN DISAPPEARANCE OF LOCAL GIRL

"We should go look for her. We'd be heroes if we found her!" Dakota interjected. Dakota always wanted to be famous. He was forever coming up with stunts and ideas to try and make the boys internet famous. His last one involved the "One Chip Challenge" on

TikTok, which got all of them grounded, one of them taken to urgent care, and two of the others puking their guts out.

"No way, what if the perv gets us??" Pedro immediately dismissed the suggestion.

"There's four of us. No way could he get us all. You're such a noob, Pedro," Jalen said, shoving Pedro in the chest.

Pedro just hung his head and mumbled, "It could be more than one."

"Where would we even start looking though?" Jalen put forth.

"We know these woods better than any grown up," Dakota replied.

"If you were some creepy perv, where would you take her?" Jalen asked.

"Oh, definitely to that old shack," Pedro piped up.

"Which one?" Jalen replied.

"The one past the railroad tracks outside of town," Pedro replied.

"How about the old mill?" Dakota chimed in.

"No way, that's right near Main Street. They've already searched there." Just then, Dakota's phone beeped.

"Shit, it's been thirty minutes. They'll notice us gone. Let's get back, and we can talk about it on Discord tonight. Eight okay?"

"Okay!" replied Jalen.

The boys climbed down out of their treehouse and made their way back. It was a good ten-minute walk from their clubhouse back to the playground.

CHAPTER TWO

It was decided later that night that the boys would look near the old house past the railroad tracks outside of town. They pulled the old "I'm going to so-and-so's house" where each kid tells his parents he's going to another kid's house. Both of Pedro's parents worked, so all the boys told their parents they would be there. Pedro said he was going to be at Jalen's house. He knew his parents wouldn't call to check, and vice versa, because his parents spoke very little English, and the other boys' parents didn't speak Spanish. Perfect.

Jalen's mom, Charlotte, was the only one who might call, but she seemed distracted with her other children when Jalen told her, so he got lucky. Dakota's and Dylan's moms knew each other and were friends. They had discussed it and decided that, even though Dakota had a tendency to get the boys into trouble, Dylan had promised they would just be playing video games. Both mothers trusted Jalen and Pedro, so it was all set.

They met at 10 a.m. so that they'd have plenty of time to make it that far and back before their parents all got home from work.

"If we find her, you can't take pics because then the cops will think we did it," Jalen told the other boys.

"Who would want to take pictures? Gross!" exclaimed Dylan.

"Who wouldn't?" Dakota replied. Seeing a dead body seemed pretty cool to him, and since they all pretty much assumed she was dead, they were expecting to see a body.

"What if we took pictures on a burner phone and hid it?" Dylan suggested.

"Who the hell has a burner phone? Do you?" Jalen laughed and looked at Dylan like he was stupid.

"Your mom does," Dylan shot back. Jalen went to smack Dylan, but missed and hit the back of Dakota's head.

"Heyyyy! I'll smash both of you!" Dakota yelled. The boys pushed and shoved playfully as they walked down the street to Pedro's house.

"You better take that back about my mama, Dylan," Jalen proclaimed as he swung and connected this time with Dylan's shoulder. "I mean it," he said, pulling back to swing again.

"Damn, okay, I take it back! Don't hit me again!" Dylan flinched.

"That's what I thought." Jaylen faked a jab, and Dylan took off running towards Pedro's house. They were only a block away. The rest of the boys took off after him.

When they got there, Pedro was coming out the front door. All of the boys ran into him and landed in a pile on the front porch, laughing and hitting each other.

"We're about to possibly go see a dead little girl. Don't you think we should be more serious?" Pedro exclaimed. Of all the boys, he was the most sensitive and felt sad for little Ruthie and her family.

"Oh, sac up, Pedro. We probably won't even find her, but if we do, you will be famous like the rest of us, and you won't even care that you saw a dead body," Dakota replied.

"I just think we should be more respectful. She's only six."

The boys all sobered up and considered what Pedro said.

"Okay, I get it, Pedro. No fooling around and making fun of whatever we see, okay guys?" Jalen looked at each one. "No one should laugh at a dead little girl. He's right."

The boys headed off to their chosen destination, careful to keep to the woods so as to avoid adult eyes. It never occurred to any of them that the kidnapper could be hiding there. Luckily for them, he was not.

They had been walking for an hour when they came upon a police search party who promptly turned them back around. With their plans foiled for the day, they decided to head to their clubhouse.

They took to the woods again and set off.

Pedro would look back on this day and recall that, as they headed further into the woods, an odd quiet came over them. First it was the cicadas, then the birds, and finally the wind. It all just stopped. He noticed it at the time, but the oddity didn't really register then.

Dakota had picked up a stick along the way and was hitting bushes. Jalen and Dylan were talking about video games. They were happily making their way to their clubhouse when Pedro noticed something gleaming from the ground ahead of them. As they got closer, the other boys passed by, but Pedro paused and studied what he was seeing. The shape was familiar, but his brain just couldn't wrap itself around what it was seeing.

He moved closer, and the air seemed to chill. That's when his brain finally caught up to his eyes, and he realized he was seeing part of an arm in the soil. He froze. As he continued staring, he realized he could also see a patch of what looked like blonde hair partially buried as well.

His stomach dropped and he yelled out, "GUYS!!!"

The other boys stopped and turned to look at Pedro, whose face had paled. He had one hand out in front of him, shaking and pointing to the ground below him. The boys immediately ran back. Once they reached Pedro, they all froze staring down at what clearly was the body of little Ruthie.

"It's her," Dylan stammered.

The boys continued to stare as if frozen to the spot. Pedro felt like he might throw up.

Dakota leaned over as if to poke the body with the stick he held.

"NO! What are you doing, Dakota?" Pedro called out in a hushed tone, as if in a funeral home. He didn't know why he didn't yell, but it just felt wrong.

"I was just going to see if it really is a body," Dakota said.

"No, that's not cool, Dakota," Jalen piped up.

"What should we do?" Pedro asked the group.

"We have to go find those cops who were searching," Jalen replied, his eyes fixed on the blonde hair showing through the dirt, but he didn't move.

The air chilled even further, and it seemed as if the sky darkened. They were four little boys alone in the woods with the tiny body of a dead little girl, and suddenly they all felt very afraid.

As Pedro continued to stare, unable to tear his eyes away, the other boys did the same. No one made a move to go get the police. It was as if they were all stuck to the spot. That's when Pedro saw it, just the tiniest of twitches from her arm. He thought to himself that he had to be seeing things.

There it was again, a small twitch, and this time a tiny hand wriggled in the dirt below the surface.

The other boys saw it as well and, as one, they all screamed and ran. Pure terror gripped them all at once, and their bodies took over, propelling them away . . . away from what their eyes had just witnessed.

Jalen was the first to stop; they had run blindly and without looking back, all the way to their treehouse. Dakota immediately started up the rope when Jalen grabbed his leg.

"Wait. Stop. We can't just leave her there, you guys," he said, seeming as if he'd just come to his senses about the magnitude of what they'd just seen.

"We have to go back," he said, looking at the other boys.

"No way! I'm not going back there!" Dylan replied, looking as if he might begin to cry.

Jalen looked at Pedro, whose eyes bore the same shine as Dylan's.

"You guys, she's alive! We have to help her!" Jalen looked at Dakota, who was staring at the ground, too afraid to do anything else.

Finally, Pedro spoke up. "Jalen's right."

"No, hell no, I'm not going back there." Dylan held firm.

"Me either." Dakota backed him up.

"Well, I'm going. Pedro, you coming?" Jalen asked and Pedro nodded. They set out back the way they had run so blindly from.

Jalen and Pedro continued to walk without speaking. Eventually, they noticed Dakota had joined them without a word. Pedro looked back and Dylan was climbing the rope into the clubhouse.

As they reached the place where they had seen the body, they edged their way up to the shallow grave's edge and were met with two big blue eyes. The girl had cleared the dirt away from her face and was just staring at them, seemingly in shock. She was just lying there looking up.

As one, the boys began to uncover her, scraping dirt and pine needles off her body. She was just a tiny little thing, so it didn't take long to uncover her. She was wearing a yellow nightgown with tiny white flowers on it. It appeared to be on backwards though, because Pedro could see the tag poking up under the girl's chin.

He spoke first.

"Ruthie? Are you okay? You want to sit up?" He stepped into the shallow grave with her and took her tiny hand. It was cold and pale. He squatted down next to her and began to sit her up. She felt hard, stiff, and it was a struggle to pull her up. All the while, those blue eyes just stared at him without speaking. He noticed a purplish red ring around her throat and winced.

"Can you talk?" Pedro asked once she was sitting up. She shook her head no and put her hands to her throat where the purple bruise was.

"We are going to go get you help, okay?" Pedro said and turned to step out of the grave, but Ruthie held tight to his hand and shook her head no again.

"You need help. You're hurt. You were buried!" Jalen said to her, and she fixed him with those blue eyes and simply shook her head once more, her eyes not leaving his.

The boys looked around at each other, confused. They were unsure and didn't know how to handle what was happening. Why didn't she want help?

She motioned for Pedro to lean down to her. He did as he was bid, and the little girl cupped her hand and whispered in his ear. Pedro nodded and listened intently. Her voice was raspy and quiet, so he had to listen carefully to hear what she was saying.

"She said that the bad man will get her again if we take her back," Pedro told the other boys. "She said she needs to hide from him."

Pedro sat back and looked at the other two boys.

"The cops will get him, Ruthie. He won't be able to hurt you anymore," Jalen said to her in the voice he used with his little sisters when they were upset.

She shook her head no again and motioned for Pedro to lean down again.

"She said . . . oh my God . . . it was her stepfather! She said no one will believe her." Pedro looked shocked, as did the other boys.

Joe Hamilton, Ruthie's stepfather, was the principal at their school. He was very well respected and well known in the community. He was on the city council and participated in any event the city was doing. He rode on a float in the Christmas parade! It was almost too much for their 12-year-old brains to comprehend.

The boys looked back and forth at each other, not sure what to think or say.

Finally, Jalen spoke.

"Ruthie, you need help. He hurt you. We can't fix you. A doctor has to do that."

Ruthie fixed him with that blue-eyed gaze and shook her head more forcefully this time, and dirt flew off her little head as she did. Then, she suddenly began to cough, and dirt flew from her mouth, landing on Pedro. He recoiled and looked horrified. She had been buried. She was coughing up dirt. She wiped her mouth off and began to get up. Pedro jumped to help her as she seemed to be struggling. He helped her out of the hole, and she began walking towards the clubhouse. The boys looked at each other and followed. Her gait was unsure and halting. Pedro had to hold her arm to keep her upright.

Who knew how long she'd been in the dirt? he thought to himself.

The air stayed unnaturally cold for June, and the clouds that had suddenly appeared, darkening the woods, remained. The boys were silent, each lost in his own thoughts, and followed little Ruthie towards the clubhouse.

So many things are wrong here, thought Pedro. It just felt wrong in so many ways, beyond the fact that they had found a missing girl and weren't running immediately to get some grown-ups. They were just kids.

As they walked, Pedro looked more closely at Ruthie. Her hair was still filled with dirt, and she had dirt smudged on her little face and nightgown. She had no socks or shoes, and her bare feet were surprisingly clean. He thought that was odd, unable to form the adult realization that she'd been carried to where she was buried. As he continued to study her, he noticed something else he did not understand. She had streaks of blood on her legs, streaks that had run down to her feet.

Was she hurt? He didn't know about that, but he did know that the marks on her neck were from being grabbed by someone there. Pedro wrestled, and he had seen similar marks on some of his teammates when a match got particularly rough. But even those weren't deep bruises like hers.

CHAPTER THREE

They managed to help her get to the clubhouse and then lifted her up gingerly through the entrance. Upon her entry, Dylan, who had been hiding inside the entire time, shrank back into a corner.

"Why did you guys bring her here? We have to go get the grown-ups!" he said with eyes almost bulging out of their sockets.

"Chill out, Dylan. She said we couldn't take her to the police because no one would believe her," Jalen replied.

"Yes, they will! This isn't something we deal with," Dylan replied.

"No, they won't. It was Mr. Hamilton, Dylan!" Pedro interjected.

The room went quiet as Dylan absorbed that information.

A full five minutes passed in silence before Dylan asked, "Well, what can we do about it? We're just kids!"

All eyes turned to Ruthie.

"What do you want us to do, Ruthie?" Pedro asked her, and she motioned for him to lean in again so she could whisper to him.

He listened intently, asked a few quiet questions, and turned back to the group.

"She said we have to prove it. She said there were cameras in the house. She's a smart little girl. If he had cameras in the house, then whatever happened would be on them, right?"

"Unless he erased them. But how are we gonna get to the cameras, Pedro?" Jalen asked him, looking very skeptical.

"Bad guys hide their shit, Pedro," Jalen continued.

"Guys, it's getting late. We're going to have to get back home. What are we going to do with Ruthie?" Dakota piped up.

"Good question. Is that good sleeping bag still here?" Being little boys, they didn't consider things like food or how to let her use the restroom. Dakota dug out the sleeping bag from the cabinet built into the walls and set it next to Ruthie.

"Can you sleep in that Ruthie?" he asked softly.

Ruthie nodded her head and motioned to Pedro again.

"She said thank you," Pedro repeated.

"This isn't right. We can't DO this, you guys," Dylan pleaded. He looked very afraid and unsure.

The other boys looked around at each other for a moment, and then Jalen said, "Look, she's just a little girl, Dylan. We have to help her. The grown-ups won't believe Mr. Hamilton did anything to her. No way. He's super popular. He's the principal!"

"You can't tell, Dylan!" Pedro said, grabbing Dylan by the arm. "We have to keep this secret. Stop being such a baby. We can do this. We'll meet back here tomorrow and figure it out."

With that, Pedro squatted down in front of Ruthie.

"You can sleep here tonight, Ruthie. You probably want to rest. I know you're tired. We'll be back in the morning and figure this out. It's gonna be okay."

Ruthie reached up with her little arms and hugged Pedro's neck. With that, the boys crawled down the rope and began to head home. Dylan immediately sprinted away from the other boys.

Dakota said, "He's going to tell, you guys. I just know he is. He's a baby. He tells his parents everything."

"He better not, or we are all screwed," Jalen responded, looking at each boy. "He's got to keep his mouth shut."

Above them, Ruthie's little face appeared in the opening of the treehouse, listening. An angry expression took over her face. Not a little girl angry expression though. It was the angry face of an adult who meant business. Her little face contorted into a mask of grim rage that only an adult can produce, and her body shook, trembling with fury.

All the boys headed to their homes with much on their minds. Pedro, Jalen, Dakota, and Dylan all went straight to their rooms. This situation was a lot for young boys to carry, to understand.

Dakota was thinking they could do it and prove Mr. Hamilton hurt Ruthie, and then be famous.

Jalen was worried about how they were going to prove what they needed to prove without getting caught. He felt a little guilty because he normally told his mother everything. They were very close, but she was a grown-up and no grown-up was going to believe Mr. Hamilton hurt his stepdaughter. Plus, he'd promised not to tell.

Meanwhile, Pedro was worrying about Ruthie being alone in the treehouse all night. He hoped she wouldn't be afraid and didn't get scared by all the noises in the woods at night. His mind swam with the heaviness of the information they had learned today. How could Mr. Hamilton do that to her? It made him afraid of him, and thought that he could come after them next.

Dylan had gone straight home and gotten in his bed without even eating dinner. He was afraid. Afraid of the whole thing and honestly? Afraid of Ruthie. Why did she look so pale? Why couldn't she talk normally? And why did she smell funny? He was so nervous that when his mother walked into his room to check on him, he jumped and yelped.

"Honey, are you not feeling well?" she asked as she sat on the corner of his bed, putting her hand on his head. "You didn't even eat supper."

"No, I'm fine," Dylan replied.

"Obviously, you aren't. You almost jumped out of your skin when I came in here. Are you upset because of the little girl that's missing? You know your dad and I won't let anything happen to you, honey." She stroked his forehead. Dylan just nodded. "Whoever did this will be caught soon. The police won't let him get away."

Dylan kept his face buried in his covers. He wanted to cry so badly. He wanted to tell her what they had found. His mom and dad would believe him. He just knew they would, but he'd promised his friends he wouldn't tell. He just wanted his parents to make this all go away. The sight of Ruthie traumatized Dylan terribly.

"Well, try to get some sleep, okay? We'll have a Mommy and Dylan Day tomorrow; we'll watch movies and eat junk food. That sound good?"

Dylan nodded his head. He just wanted to sit with his mom and feel like everything was okay.

As she left the room, Dylan lay back in his bed and began to convince himself that he should tell his parents. He lay there arguing back and forth in his own head. It was too much for a 12-year-old to handle. His young brain didn't know what to do.

He rolled over to his left side and stared out his window. Dusk was just passing, and it was starting to get dark. He thought of Ruthie in the treehouse and shuddered. Something felt wrong with all of this to him.

He had just about decided to get up and go tell his parents when he heard something tap his bedroom glass. Lying there in the dark, Dylan was immediately afraid. He sat up in his bed and squinted, trying to see out the window. He knew he'd heard something tap his glass. As he peered at the window, a small face appeared. It was Ruthie . . . but it wasn't.

Her face was about an inch from the window. She was as pale as she'd been before, and he could still see clumps of dirt in her hair and smeared on her face. But it was her eyes that made Dylan's heart skip a beat. They were glowing yellowish, like when you shine a flashlight on a cat's eyes. Panic and fear made Dylan scream a bloodcurdling scream. Ruthie's face remained there. She blinked her glowing eyes and brought her tiny finger up to her mouth in a "Shhh" motion, and then the window faded black. She was gone by the time his parents burst through his doorway.

"What's wrong, buddy?" his dad asked him as he flicked on the bedroom light.

Dylan's eyes immediately darted back to the window. Nothing. He was hysterical, pointing to the window and saying, "She's there! She's out there!"

"Who? Who's out there?" His dad walked to the window and peered out. "Buddy, there's no one out there," he said.

"Ruthie! It was Ruthie!" Dylan gasped out between his rapid panting breaths.

"Oh, honey, you thought you saw Ruthie?" asked his mom. "She's not out there. You're just upset about this whole situation. We all are, but Ruthie wasn't outside your window. The police are looking for her. I told you that, remember? They will find her." She turned to her husband. "I think he's really upset about Ruthie being missing. It's just really affecting him."

"I think your mom's right, buddy. This is scary for everyone. I think your imagination just got carried away because you have all the worry about Ruthie in your head," he said to his crying son.

"You want to sleep in the living room on the couch with the TV on?" his mother offered. That was a big deal. She never offered that.

He nodded his head, and they grabbed his blankets and pillow. Once they had him set up on the couch with SpongeBob on the TV, they both kissed him and headed back to bed. Dylan lay there trembling. He knew what he saw, and he also knew he wasn't going to say a word to anyone about Ruthie. He was not going back to that treehouse.

~ ~ ~

Around the same time, Dakota was looking out his window across the street from Dylan's house, wondering if Dylan was telling his parents and waiting for the phone to ring at his house with his mom calling. As he stared outside, he saw a dark shape move towards Dylan's window. There wasn't enough light for him to see any details, but it was definitely a person. The dark shape moved to Dylan's window for just a few seconds, and then backed away.

Just before the figure started into the woods, it turned its head towards him, as if it could sense him looking at it. Dakota saw a pair of glowing eyes and immediately propelled himself back from his window.

What was that?!

He leaned back towards the window, but the figure was gone.

CHAPTER FOUR

Ruthie made her way back into the woods.

She had other business this evening.

Three houses down from Dylan's house was the home of Ms. Skinner, Ruthie's teacher.

Ms. Skinner, who saw bruises on Ruthie's body.

Ms. Skinner, who wouldn't ask the questions that needed to be asked.

Ms. Skinner, who didn't report what she had seen when Ruthie told her that her bottom hurt, and she couldn't sit on the wooden chairs in the music room.

Ms. Skinner, who just shushed her and sent her to the school nurse.

Yes, she needed a visit.

~ ~ ~

Ms. Skinner was sitting on her couch drinking her fifth glass of wine that night. She had been drinking too much since Ruthie disappeared. No, that wasn't true. Martha Skinner had been drinking too much since she saw the bruises and the way Ruthie sat uncomfortably on the chairs in the music room. She knew she should have reported her observations. She was a mandatory reporter, after all, but she did nothing. She didn't want to make any waves that might cause her to lose her job. She was too close to retirement.

I mean, what could I really have done? she asked herself, trying to assuage the guilt that had been creeping in since Ruthie's disappearance. She knew nothing for sure, or who, if anyone, caused the bruises. They could have just been from playing too rough outside. Surely the little girl is just hiding somewhere around town. They'll find her. At least school is out for the summer, and she was out of the situation. She hoped.

Her little dog, Cozmo, started barking like crazy at the back sliding glass doors.

"What are you barking at? There's nothing out there, Cozmo. Come back over here, you silly dog," Ms. Skinner said, trying to get her dog away from the doors, but the dog wouldn't move. She seemed to be getting more worked up by the second, her eyes glued to the sliding glass doors, her little body trembling.

Martha stood up to gather the dog up and away from the doors. At that moment, Cozmo let out a squeal and ran under the table whining.

"Cozmo, what has gotten into you? You peed! Shame on you!" Martha scolded him as she went to the door to see what had scared Cozmo. Probably a fox. She'd seen a few recently on the edge of the woods. As she approached the door, she thought she saw a shadow move, and a chill came over her.

"Hello! Is someone out there?" she called out as she approached. Her hand was on the handle when she froze.

There, on her patio, stood Ruthie.

Martha paused a few seconds more and then jerked the sliding glass door open.

"Oh my God, Ruthie! Are you okay? Where have you been?" she asked as she grabbed the child and pulled her into the house. Ruthie was freezing cold to the touch. Poor child must have been lost in the woods.

"Let me get you a blanket."

She ran to the couch, grabbed her blanket, and threw it over Ruthie's shoulders. Ruthie just stared at her, not saying a word.

"Here, honey, sit in this chair," she said as she pulled a chair from the table. Ruthie continued to stare silently as she guided her tiny body into the chair.

She realized she needed to call the police. The poor child must be in shock. She turned to go get her phone when she felt a firm but small hand on her wrist. She looked at Ruthie, confused; her grip was hurting her.

"Ruthie, honey, you're okay now. You are safe. Let go of Ms. Skinner's arm now so that I can call for help," she said, as the pressure on her wrist increased.

"Ow, dear, that's too hard. You're hurting me."

Ruthie continued to stare straight into Ms. Skinner's eyes, not releasing her grip. She didn't say a word, just kept hold of Ms. Skinner's wrist.

Martha looked, really looked, at Ruthie's pale skin and bruised neck. Ruthie was extremely gaunt; her eyes were sunken into her head to the point that her cheekbones were abnormally pronounced. Her lips were cracked, and, more startling, her hair looked patchy, almost as if it was falling out.

It began to dawn on her that something was very wrong. She tried to pull her wrist free, but couldn't. Cozmo continued to whine under the table, and the room chilled.

"Ruthie, I . . ." Ms. Skinner began to crumble under the weight of Ruthie's accusing gaze and the pain in her wrist.

"Ruthie, honey, you have to understand that if I knew, *really* knew anything, I would have helped you," she suddenly blurted out. "I mean how could I know for certain anything was wrong? It would have just caused trouble for both of us."

Ruthie tightened her grip to the point that Ms. Skinner dropped to her knees weeping with her head down. Ruthie leaned forward then and lifted Ms. Skinner's chin so that their eyes met. Ruthie's eyes were glowing.

Martha continued to blubber about not knowing and eventually began to sob that she was sorry.

But it was too late for sorry.

Ruthie removed her hand from Ms. Skinner's wrist and put both her little hands around her throat, knocking her backwards onto the floor at the same time. Ruthie's eyes began to glow brighter, and Ms. Skinner began to panic.

Ruthie could see it in her eyes.

She clawed at Ruthie's hands and managed to dislodge one, but Ruthie used that hand to grab hold of Ms. Skinner's jaw. She jerked her mouth open so wide her jaw began to separate from its joints with an audible pop. She barely managed to choke out screams from the pain. Ruthie sat straddling the still screaming woman's chest. She cocked her head sideways like a bird to study her teacher's reddened face, her glowing eyes unblinking.

"Why didn't you help me?"

Ruthie reached her grimy hands into the pockets of her dainty nightgown, now stained with dirt and blood, and produced two fistfuls of dirt. Ms. Skinner's eyes widened at the sight. She shoved one handful of dirt into Ms. Skinner's mouth and then another. One after another, she crammed the dirt into her mouth, shoving it down, down, down, until Ruthie's tiny fists were halfway in the woman's throat. Time after time she reached into those pockets of her pretty little gown to pull out more of the dirt that had buried her small, broken body.

Ms. Skinner struggled and choked, trying to dislodge the dirt, but it was no use.

Ruthie was now strong in death, something she had never been in life.

Ms. Skinner's eyes bulged as her body fought for air that wasn't coming. Ruthie kept cramming the dirt into her throat, shoving her tiny hands deeper into the vile woman's gullet. Her stomach began to distend. Soon, she was nothing but a meat sack filled with dirt. A single maggot wriggled its way out of the dirt in her mouth and crawled onto her cheek. Her eyes rolled back in her head, and she succumbed to her fate.

Ruthie's face was a mixture of rage and sadness. Tears made tracks down her dirty face, and snot ran from her little nose.

When she was all out of dirt and rage, the woman was no longer moving. Ruthie stood up from the carcass, wiped her nose on her sleeve, and turned towards the dog who had stopped barking and sat watching the spectacle from a few feet away.

Ruthie got down on her knees and patted her lap, encouraging the dog to come to her. He came without hesitation. She pulled the tiny dog into her lap and began to pet him. She had always wanted a dog but had never been allowed to have one. Cozmo licked her face and wiggled in delight. Ruthie giggled.

She sat stroking the dog for ten full minutes. Then went into the kitchen where she found his food bag and poured it all out onto the floor. With one last pat on his head, she turned to leave, without sparing a glance at one of the adults who had failed her. She would never fail another child.

CHAPTER FIVE

The next morning, the boys all woke up early and headed to Pedro's house. None of them had any idea of what had occurred at Dylan's house or at Ms. Skinner's house.

"Where's Dylan?" Pedro asked Dakota.

"He's not coming. His mom said he was sick," Dakota answered, shrugging his shoulders.

"Do you think he told?" Jalen asked Dakota, looking concerned.

"No, or his mom would have said something to me for sure," Dakota replied.

"Okay guys, let's head out. We need to bring some food for her. We didn't leave her anything last night." Pedro held up a grocery bag full of snacks he'd pilfered from the cabinets.

"I have some Gatorade in my backpack," Dakota offered up.

"Okay, good. Let's go," Pedro replied.

The boys headed out into the woods, again having told their parents they were hanging at Pedro's house for the day.

The day was gray and overcast, and as they got closer to the clubhouse, the temperature dropped, but none of the boys noticed.

They found Ruthie where they'd left her, sitting in the corner of the treehouse in a sleeping bag. She beamed a huge smile at all of them, making them all smile back.

"We brought you some snacks, Ruthie," Pedro said as he handed her the bag of goodies. She grabbed it and immediately dumped it all out in front of her, looking delighted. She had Pop-Tarts, Fruit Roll-Ups, a bag of Cheerios, some cheese and crackers, and other kids' snacks. She ripped open a granola bar and began wolfing it down.

"I'm sorry we forgot to leave you food yesterday, Ruthie," Jalen said, putting his hand on her shoulder. Somewhere in the back of his mind, he noted how cold she was to the touch.

Pedro pulled out some wet wipes and handed them to Ruthie.

"You have some dirt around your mouth, and your hands are really dirty, Ruthie. Why don't you wipe them off?"

She did as she was told and went back to eating.

The boys plopped down on the floor with their backpacks and sat quietly while she ate.

At some point, Jalen pulled out his Nintendo Switch and began playing. The rest of the boys did the same, and all sat in a comfortable silence playing their games while Ruthie ate. It all seemed so normal, just kids doing what kids do. It was almost like they didn't have this huge issue hanging over them: a missing girl sitting in their treehouse and no idea what to do from here.

Ruthie finished up her food and sat quietly watching the boys play, seeming content.

Jalen noticed she was finished and offered to let her play his game. She went over and sat right next to him, shoulder to shoulder. Again, Jalen noticed the coldness radiating off her body.

"Are you cold?" he asked her. She shook her head no and happily took his gaming device and began playing.

While she played, Jalen motioned the other boys over to the corner of the clubhouse.

"Guys, we have to come up with a plan. I've been thinking a lot about what Ruthie said about the cameras, and I think I have an idea." Jalen was the tech whiz in the group. He fancied himself to be a hacker and knew more about tech than any of the other boys. He'd once gotten in trouble at school for hacking the school website and posting that school was canceled.

"I think I can hack into the home security camera system, but I have to be close to the house," Jalen continued.

"How are we going to get close? I don't want Mr. Hamilton to see us. He might kill us too!" Dakota proclaimed.

"He's dangerous for sure," Pedro agreed.

"They are holding a candlelight thing out in front of his house tonight. If we go, I think I can get my laptop close enough to the house to hack their system and download the camera recordings," Jalen said, looking excited. "Then, we can prove what happened, and the police will believe us and help Ruthie. I need to know what day he, uh . . . when everything happened. Pedro, can you ask Ruthie? Then I can get a couple days before and after."

Jalen looked at Pedro and he nodded.

Pedro sat down next to Ruthie.

"Ruthie, we are trying to help you, okay?" Ruthie nodded her little head and looked at Pedro wide-eyed. "I need to ask you some questions, and it might be hard to remember, but try your best."

Ruthie nodded her head again.

"Remember when we found you?" he asked, and she whispered "Yes" in her hoarse voice. "How many days before that did your stepdad put you in that hole. Do you remember?"

Her eyes filled with tears and Pedro instantly regretted upsetting the girl.

"I know it's hard, Ruthie, but it's important. Can you remember how many times it got dark and then the day came while you were there?"

Ruthie leaned in to whisper to Pedro, and in the tiniest voice she said, "I think it was four or maybe three. I was afraid and can't remember."

A tear rolled down her pale cheek and Pedro hugged the girl to him and told her she had done good. She went back to playing her game.

"Well?" Jalen asked when Pedro returned.

"She was really scared, you guys, and she's just a little girl. She thinks it was three or four days before we found her that he put her there."

"Okay, that's good enough. I'll do two days before that and two days after," Jalen said.

They spent the remainder of the afternoon playing video games in the clubhouse. Funny how children can compartmentalize such an enormous situation, but they were just being kids. Games were safe and didn't require thinking about the unknown or scary things. Ruthie played along with them and acted like any other six-year-old girl. The boys were all good kids. They were kind to her, brotherly, and taught her how to play their games. They didn't even get angry when she killed a character.

Pedro noticed more and more how gaunt Ruthie seemed. Jalen had little sisters and brothers, and he didn't recall any of them looking that gaunt. A couple of hours into the day, he left the boys to run back to his home and get more food and drink to leave there with Ruthie. Being 12, he convinced himself she just needed more to eat.

Once Pedro returned with the food and some extra blankets and pillows, the boys decided they had better leave before Pedro's parents got home from work. Ruthie was stoic as they piled blankets in the corner and left her the mounds of snacks.

"We've got stuff to do tonight, Ruthie, to try and catch your stepdad. You just stay here and lay low. If anyone comes to the clubhouse, just stay quiet. If they come up the rope, there's a box in the corner under that seat." Jalen pointed to the seat in the right corner of the room that opened up into a storage area. "You can get in there, if you need to, okay?" She nodded her head yes, fixing him with those big blue eyes.

"There's nothing to be afraid of, Ruthie. We got you. Most adults can't climb that rope anyway," Dakota added.

"We'll find out what happened, and then you can go home to your mom once the police have your stepdad," Pedro said, assuming she, of course, wanted her mom.

But Ruthie had no intention of returning to her mother. Her mother, who suspected something was wrong. The mother who stood by while her stepfather physically abused her and did nothing, because she didn't want to be alone or give up her standing in the community. No, she had other plans for her "mother."

The boys left, went to their respective homes, and told their parents they wanted to go to the candlelight vigil that night. Of course, their parents agreed. The whole town was going.

Each boy retreated to his room and jumped on Discord.

"Okay guys, the plan is that I'll bring my laptop to the vigil, and we'll sit in the grass near Mr. Hamilton's house like we are just watching the vigil," Jalen said. He felt sure he could get what they needed. He hadn't found a network he couldn't hack, and home security cameras were the easiest.

"What if he sees us?" Pedro asked.

"It won't matter, Pedro. He'll just think we are sitting together taking video of the vigil," Jalen replied. He was confident in his plan.

Dylan hopped on.

"Where have you been Dylan?" Jalen asked him immediately. "We are going to the vigil tonight to try and get the camera footage from Ruthie's house. Why weren't you at the treehouse today? We need to solve this. We need to help Ruthie."

Dylan remained silent for a moment and then said, "I can't go, you guys. My mom says I have to stay here."

"What? Everyone in the town is going. What is the deal, Dylan? Did you tell your parents about Ruthie?" Jalen asked.

"No! I swear I didn't. I, uh, I've just not been feeling well."

"I call bullshit," Dakota popped in.

"No, really guys. I haven't been sleeping and stuff," Dylan replied immediately. "I . . . just don't feel like going out, but I haven't said anything to anyone. I swear."

"Why are you being so weird?" Dakota asked him.

"I'm not. Please don't tell Ruthie," Dylan almost shouted.

"Tell Ruthie? Tell Ruthie what? What is your problem with Ruthie, Dylan? You're being a puss," Jalen said, starting to get pissed at Dylan.

"N-nothing. I don't have a problem with Ruthie. Look, I gotta go," Dylan said and promptly got offline.

"What was that all about?" Jalen asked Dakota.

"No idea, but you know Dylan gets scared easily."

"He better not blow this, or we're all be in shit," Jalen said.

"He won't. I'll talk to him later tonight," Dakota assured Jalen.

Jalen didn't trust that Dylan wouldn't tell his parents. He hoped Dakota could talk some sense into him.

CHAPTER SIX

The vigil was held in front of the Hamiltons' home in the cul-de-sac. The entire town was there, all the adults looking somber, some were crying. There was a memorial set up near the mailbox of Mr. Hamilton's house. People had brought teddy bears, cards, flowers, and there were handwritten notes from the children in Ruthie's class in children's scrawl. Some had drawn pictures and made cards. Parents seemed to cling to their children in the face of such a terrifying and heartbreaking event. People held hands and hugged one another. Even the smallest of children seemed to sense the sadness and remained quiet, studying the faces of the adults to try and understand.

The boys arrived with their families and quickly separated to meet up.

"Okay, we have to get closer to the house," Jalen said, holding his laptop in his right hand and a candle in the other. Pedro had said they all needed to take a candle so they would blend in.

As the minister began to speak, the boys made their way to the corner of the grass and sat down in a group as if they were listening. Jalen handed his candle to Pedro and began working.

Jalen was always on a computer or iPad of some kind, so no one thought it out of place to see him with one now. The other boys looked around at the crowd to make sure no one was watching them closely, especially Mr. Hamilton. The boys looked at him with fear and trepidation, knowing what he had done. It was hard to process that an adult they all trusted could do something so awful, and it left them with a healthy fear of the man.

As the minister finished speaking, the crowd began to sing "Amazing Grace."

"Okay, I'm in, downloading the footage now," Jalen whispered.

Just then, Mr. Hamilton seemed to notice the boys and made his way over to them. The boys froze. Jalen tilted the laptop screen away from him.

"Boys," Mr. Hamilton said and made, what seemed to them, a pathetic attempt at a tired smile, looking at each of them. "Thank you so much for coming. It means a lot to my wife and me. Maybe you'd like to join the rest of the crowd." He indicated they needed to get off his grass with one leveled look.

"Yes, sir, we were just videotaping from here because we can see everyone," Jalen quickly answered. He could feel Pedro trembling next to him. Dakota's eyes were huge, and he just stared at Mr. Hamilton.

"The police told me they met you boys out in the woods looking for Ruthie the other day."

This caught all the boys off guard. How did he know that? "And while I truly appreciate you boys trying to help, you really shouldn't go into the woods alone like that. We don't know who took our Ruthie, and it could be dangerous out there for little boys." He stared each one in the eyes after he said it, giving the statement an undercurrent of warning.

"Yes, sir. The police told us the same. We were just trying to help," said Jalen. Pedro was still frozen and trembling, as was Dakota.

"Well, we don't want to lose anyone else, Jalen, so make sure you boys stay out of the woods and let the police do the searching."

He turned to go join his wife, who had just stepped up to the microphone.

"Done. Got it." Jalen closed the laptop case, and the boys all went to join their families in the crowd. Dakota still looked like he might cry, and Pedro was pale as a ghost. No one noticed because everyone there was upset.

What did he know? Pedro wondered to himself. Did he KNOW? No, if he did, he'd have already killed us, he concluded.

Meanwhile, Jalen was having similar thoughts. That man was dirty. He knew that in his bones, and they'd have to watch their backs from here on out. He couldn't wait to go through the footage and hopefully nail that asshole.

As the vigil began to wrap up, Jalen's mom handed him the youngest of his three sisters and asked what Mr. Hamilton had said to them. Jalen assured her he was just thanking them for coming.

"Y'all don't bother that man or go near him. He has a lot on his mind," she said to Jalen as they began to leave.

"We weren't bothering him. I swear," Jalen replied.

"I know you weren't. I'd just prefer that you stay away from him, Jalen."

Suddenly, Jalen realized his mother was looking at Mr. Hamilton with something that wasn't sympathy. Did she suspect something? His mother had been in an abusive relationship and had a general distrust of men. He wondered if she had a feeling about Mr. Hamilton. He wished just then that he could tell her everything. It wasn't like him to keep secrets from her, but he'd promised the guys and Ruthie. No adults were to be involved.

His mother put her hand on his shoulder, as if reading his thoughts, and said, "Something isn't right here, Jalen, and I'd feel better if you just stayed away from Mr. Hamilton altogether. School is out, so there should be no reason for you to be around him. Let the police handle this, and you keep your distance." With that, she led the family away and back towards home.

She did suspect something! He knew it! His mother was smart and had a sense about people.

All the more reason to help Ruthie bust him and get him put away forever, Jalen thought.

~ ~ ~

On the other side of town, as the night deepened, Ruthie climbed down from the treehouse. Her eyes were more sunken and her limbs stiffer.

She didn't have much time.

She walked towards town, keeping to the woods to avoid eyes and keeping away from where she could hear the sounds of the search party, which had started back up.

Ruthie moved towards the home of Mr. Snyder, her bus driver. She had really loved Mr. Snyder and had once trusted him enough to show him a set of bruises on her legs one morning after she got on the bus. He asked her what happened, and she explained that she had gotten in trouble at home for not finishing her food that night. The bruises were dark, but the welts were worse. She expected him to be shocked, to be outraged, and to help her. She could barely walk that day. Instead, he told her to put her dress down and listen to her parents when they told her to do something. Then he mentioned something about "sparing the rod and spoiling the child." She didn't know what that meant, but she knew he wasn't going to help her.

When she got home that night, somehow her stepfather knew she had spoken to Mr. Snyder. He had betrayed her, and the consequences were terrifying. She'd spent the night with a rag in her mouth to remind her not to talk and kneeling on dry rice to remind her who was in charge of that house, who the "king" of that castle was. She was made to kneel before him on the rice with the rag in her mouth and then, well, then other things happened that her mind kept blacking out, but she knew it was bad. Her brain didn't seem to be remembering things very well, and mostly what she felt was anger and a thirst for revenge.

Ruthie approached Mr. Snyder's garage from the rear and saw him through the window. He was drinking a beer with the radio playing as he tinkered with something on a workbench. He was a man in his 60s with a long gray beard and gray hair. He wore a pair of faded overalls and a white t-shirt. She stood watching him for a few minutes. Her eyes began to glow, and her lips curled back in a snarl. The sounds of country music swirled in the air, making the hiss that escaped her lips almost impossible to hear. She smelled of urine, dirt, and something else . . . decay. Her yellow nightgown was filthy, as were her legs, face, and arms. Her hair was a matted mess, and she still had pieces of leaves in it.

Mr. Snyder was singing along to the radio and then suddenly stopped, seeming to sense that he was being watched. He looked towards the garage window, and Ruthie stepped into the light illuminating from it. He saw her, eyes aglow, thin as a rail, and looking like a walking corpse. Her mouth curled back into a wicked and terrifying smile. She raised one tiny arm and pointed at him.

Mr. Snyder did not rush to her aid as Ms. Skinner had. He dropped his beer and began to back up, his mouth frozen in a scream that would not come. He turned to grab something from his workbench, perhaps to defend himself with, and at the same time uttered, "Oh God, no. Please help me."

But Ruthie was through the glass window and on him before he could grab whatever he was reaching for. She climbed up his back and tore at him like a feral beast, biting and scratching. He stumbled around the garage, trying to dislodge her, still not screaming, but desperately trying to escape her grasp.

He could smell the death on her as she tore at him, and it just increased his panic. No thoughts entered his head. He was acting purely out of self-preservation. He managed to get ahold of her hair and fling her off his back. His hand came away with a large maggot-filled clump of hair. Ruthie was on all fours and hissed at him like an angry feline. She began to bear crawl towards him, her intensely glowing eyes fixed on him.

Mr. Snyder turned and ran towards the bus that was parked in his driveway. He only made it to the door before Ruthie was back on him, tearing at his throat with her nails. He began to bleed as she dug deeper and deeper. His flesh tore beneath her supernaturally strong clawing fingers. Blood began to pour from his throat, and then she replaced her filthy, clawed little hands with her teeth and began tearing at his throat. Blood began gushing then, and it covered his shirt and Ruthie's face. Her eyes glowed brightly.

The bus door was open, and he began to try to drag himself up the steps with Ruthie on his back. Before he could get past the first step, Ruthie jumped off him and climbed up to the platform near the driver's seat.

Then, in the most innocent of voices, she said hoarsely, "I trusted you, Mr. Snyder. Why didn't you help me?"

A tiny tear made its way down her cheek as she pulled the door handle, trapping him by the neck in the bus door. She walked down the steps and squatted down, her face an inch from his. With one quick movement, she bit into his lips with her teeth and began thrashing her head left to right, ripping the flesh from his face. She jammed her thumbs into his eyes and pushed with all her might until she heard slight pops and felt the gooey insides of his eyes running over her fingers.

Ruthie got up and turned back towards the door lever. Her bloody little hands had some trouble gripping it, but eventually she had a good hold of it. She opened and closed it repeatedly, splattering blood on the window and herself. Each thud of the door on his limp body produced a spray of blood from his bloody, mangled mouth.

She kept pushing and pulling the handle until he stopped moving, then got down on the bottom step and squatted over him once again. He was gurgling deep in his throat.

"You should have helped me," she uttered and then stepped over his body and walked slowly back towards the woodline.

Mr. Snyder lay there choking on his own blood, dying. His neck was ripped open and his face smashed from the door. He had slid down onto the pavement once she opened the door. His one good arm reached out as if to try and drag himself up the stairs, but he would not be going anywhere. His last thoughts were pleading with God to help him.

As if she could hear them, Ruthie stopped, turned to face him, and said, "There is no God here, Mr. Snyder."

~ ~ ~

Jalen got home and had to help with his siblings, so he didn't get to review the footage. Plus, he was exhausted after so much adrenaline had pumped through his body from coming face to face with Mr. Hamilton. Off to bed Jalen went, and in the living room his laptop sat. It was because of that oversight that Charlotte, Jalen's mother, happened to spot it. She kept a close eye on her kids, and after Jalen got into trouble in school for hacking the school webpage (which she laughed about with her friends but not with him), she watched him a bit closer.

She picked up his laptop and typed in his passcode. That was one of the stipulations to keeping his electronics after the school webpage incident. She perused through his search history and photos, the usual stuff. She was about to close the laptop when she noticed a folder named "Hamilton_house1" and immediately clicked on it. There were dozens of media files.

What was he up to? she wondered. She was instantly concerned when she saw that name on her son's computer. It just took watching a few clips for her to realize what her son had done. He'd hacked Joe Hamilton's home security cameras! She didn't even have to wonder what he was looking for, and her heart dropped. That must have been what he and his friends were doing sitting on Joe's lawn during the vigil.

Charlotte went into the kitchen to grab a glass of wine. She paced back and forth trying to decide what she should do. That child was playing a dangerous game, and she was sure he didn't even realize how dangerous. Too smart for his own good, that one. He was just like his mom; he could read people like a book. He must have suspected exactly what she'd been suspecting all along about Joe Hamilton. He was involved in his stepdaughter's disappearance.

She knew she'd have to look, and that's what she did. The fact that she had to get up early for work did not even enter her mind. She had to know.

~ ~ ~

Meanwhile, Ruthie was making her way back to the treehouse and decided to stop by Dylan's house to make sure he'd kept his promise to keep her secret to himself. She found him sitting in his room in front of the TV playing a video game. She walked up to the glass and watched him long enough for him to feel her presence. She knew the minute he sensed her and could see him wrestling with his fear. His curiosity finally won out and he turned to look out of the window.

What he saw there was Ruthie's tiny face and glowing eyes watching him. He froze.

Ruthie motioned for him to approach the window and, like a robot, he did. When he was about two feet from the window, she said, "Hi Dylan," in her scratchy, quiet voice. "Please don't be afraid of me."

He just stood there staring. He noticed she was dirtier than before and had what looked like blood on her face. She was also missing a patch of hair from the side of her head.

"I won't hurt you. I promise. I just need you to keep our secret, okay?"

Dylan simply nodded.

"Thank you, Dylan. I knew you were my friend. You are my friend, right?" she asked the frightened boy.

"Y-yes. I guess," Dylan replied, still scared out of his mind. It was her appearance, and she knew it.

"Dylan. Someone hurt me really bad. Can you see that?"

"Yeah," Dylan replied.

"Don't you think they deserve to be punished?"

"Yeah, I do."

"Good. I know you don't like how I look, and it scares you, so I understand why you aren't coming to the clubhouse any longer. I'm not mad. I just need you to promise you won't tell anyone about me so that the other boys can help me. Okay?"

"Okay," Dylan agreed, and with that, Ruthie faded away from the window, and Dylan dropped to the floor, his controller landing on the hardwood and making a loud "thunk" noise.

That prompted his mother to yell, "Dylan, don't throw your controller, or I'll take it away." She thought he was losing his temper at his game.

Dylan swallowed the bile in his throat and yelled back, "Sorry, Mom!"

CHAPTER SEVEN

The boys had a soccer clinic the next day and plans to stay the night at Dakota's house that night. Jalen's mom woke him up at 6:30 a.m. to begin getting ready. She always made sure he ate a good breakfast before starting his day. This was the same routine they had during the school year.

Jalen had three sisters: Jasmine (6), Octavia (3), and baby Shantelle (1). His mother and father had split up before Shantelle was born, and shortly after, they moved to Lakeview. His mother had said they needed a fresh start in a new part of the country. So, from New Jersey to Georgia they had moved into a three-bedroom house in the same subdivision as Dakota, Dylan, and Pedro. The baby's crib was in his mother's room. The older girls shared another room, and Jalen had his own room. Jalen's grandmother and other family lived about 20 miles away, one town over.

Charlotte was the office manager at a doctor's office in town where Dakota's mothers both worked. That is how they became friends. Jalen had no trouble adjusting to his new town and school. It was much smaller and the kids friendlier than where they had lived before. Jalen was a confident, funny, and smart boy who easily made friends. It didn't hurt that the kids looked at him as sort of a novelty, having lived in a large city before. Jalen, Dakota, Pedro, and Dylan had become fast friends and were pretty much inseparable. Where you found one, you found the others. He was excited about the soccer clinic, but more so for the sleepover that was to come.

After he ate breakfast, his mother reminded him to pack clothes and not just his game controllers. He rolled his eyes but grabbed the expected clothing items. When he went into the living room to grab his laptop, he noticed a wine glass sitting next to it. He froze and looked over at his mother standing in the kitchen, hoping she hadn't looked through it. He quietly shoved it into his backpack.

Charlotte had noticed him getting his laptop out of the corner of her eye, but said nothing. She still had not decided what to do with the memory stick containing the files she had copied from it. She hadn't gone through them all yet.

The same activities were happening at Dakota's house—breakfast, gathering of gear and, for him, the cleaning of his room for the sleepover. His mothers were Christine and Megan, known as Mom and Momma Meg. Dakota never knew his father. He had only ever known Momma Meg. She'd entered his life when he was just a baby. A gay couple wasn't the norm in his small southern town, but, for the most part, Dakota didn't have a lot of problems with the other kids at school.

The only time an issue occurred had been this year, during his first year of middle school in seventh grade. That's what bonded him and Jalen so closely. Jalen had jumped into the fray and clapped back at the boys giving Dakota a hard time. He gave them such brutal verbal takedowns that they had never opened their mouths to Dakota again. Pedro was there too, fists clenched and ready to fight, but it wasn't necessary. It was nice to know that he would have, though.

He was getting his gear ready when his mom (Christine) sat down on the couch across from him.

"Dakota, Dylan's mom called me this morning to say he wasn't coming. Did you two have a fight?"

"No, Mom. I promise."

Dakota and Dylan had known each other since kindergarten and lived across the street from each other. Dakota knew why Dylan wasn't coming, but he wasn't about to tell his mother that.

"I'm going to call his mom back and try to convince her to try and talk him into coming. I know she said he's been very on edge since Ruthie disappeared. Has he said anything to you?"

"Nope," Dakota answered in a typically dismissive 12-year-old boy speak.

"Well, you guys be easy with him. His mom told me he's having nightmares and has been very upset."

"Okaaaay, Mom," Dakota answered, getting irritated with the whole conversation. Truth be told, he was a little pissed with Dylan for bailing on them in their quest to help little Ruthie.

His mom gave him "the look," and he changed his tone and answered, "I promise. We won't bring it up or scare him, geez."

"I know the situation with Ruthie is upsetting whether you admit it or not," his mother continued the conversation. "It's a scary thing for all of us, but you know that you are safe, right? Momma Meg and I won't let anything happen to you." She reached out and patted him on his leg.

Dakota rolled his eyes and said, "Yessss, Moooom."

Just then Momma Meg chimed in, "This is serious, Dakota. Stop acting like a tough guy and listen."

"It's sad and scary the way she just disappeared, but I'm not afraid. I know not to talk to strangers, not to go off alone, and I have the boys. We're a pretty sick crew. *I* wouldn't mess with us."

"All the same, don't walk around afraid, but be aware. Okay?"

"Okay, Mom. I promise."

She hugged Dakota and turned back to finish fixing his breakfast in the kitchen.

~ ~ ~

"It feels strange to just be going on with our lives while someone's child is missing," Christine said to Meg as they made breakfast.

Meg was putting the pancakes on the griddle while Christine was cutting up fruit.

"It does. I can't imagine what the Hamiltons are going through. Have you heard of any more search parties?"

"It was Charlotte who told me she heard that the police were calling in other agencies and handling all the searches. I don't think they are holding out much hope that she's alive and that's so sad."

Christine teared up just thinking about the absolute torment the Hamiltons must be feeling. She couldn't imagine what she'd do if Dakota went missing. She knew she'd be out searching day and night.

"I'm kind of surprised that Joe wasn't at any of the searches or out looking," Meg said while flipping a pancake.

"I was just thinking the same thing. Maybe the police told him to stay home?"

"No one could keep me from looking for my child," Meg said, glancing over at Dakota, who was busy putting his shin guards on. She knew she wouldn't just sit at home and trust others to find her own child. Come to think of it, she hadn't seen Elaine Hamilton, Ruthie's mother, since the candlelight vigil.

Christine and I really aren't close enough to Elaine to pop by and check on her, but maybe we ought to take her a casserole, she thought to herself.

"Maybe we should take Elaine some food? We could take her a casserole. Do you think that's a good idea?" she asked.

"That's a great idea. We can make it while the boys are doing their thing tonight and take it over tomorrow," suggested Christine.

CHAPTER EIGHT

It was much quieter at Pedro's house. His mother and father had both left at 5 a.m. for work. Pedro set out shortly after that to take Ruthie some food and check on her. He could hear the sounds of birds chirping and chattering, squirrels hopping through the leaves, and a random dog barking now and then. That was until he approached the spot where they had found Ruthie partially buried. It was like some kind of demarcation line in the woods. All animal noises seemed to stop there, the air chilled, and the light, barely coming over the horizon, seemed to dim. As Pedro approached the treehouse, for the first time since all of this with Ruthie had started, he felt hesitation—not quite fear but something akin to it.

He climbed up the rope and found Ruthie asleep, buried under blankets and sleeping bags. Pedro couldn't even see her, but he knew she was there. He approached slowly, not wanting to scare the girl.

"Ruthie. It's Pedro."

No response.

"Ruthie, wake up. I came to bring you some food and to check on you."

Pedro moved closer to the pile of blankets. It was then that he noticed a slightly foul odor coming from them. He thought Ruthie probably needed a bath after being this long in the woods. He had brought some wet wipes with him to offer her.

Pedro kneeled down next to the pile of blankets and reached gently for Ruthie's leg. Before his hand even touched her, he was suddenly face to face with a crouched, hissing, wild creature with glowing yellow eyes. He hadn't seen or felt her move. She was just there. Her eyes were wide and unblinking, drool dripped from her drawn-back mouth, exposing yellowed teeth and rotting gray gums. She was pale and filthy dirty, her face smudged with dirt, her nails caked with it and something brownish red. There were faded crimson stains on the tips of her fingers. She had a bald patch on the left side of her head, as if the hair had just fallen out. The smell Pedro had noticed earlier was now more pronounced. It was awful and something he had smelled before but couldn't quite place. Her tiny legs were marred with scratches and spots that looked bruised, as was the side of her face.

Pedro propelled himself backwards and landed on his butt. Ruthie was instantly on top of him, teeth bared, patchy hair akimbo from sleeping. She had murder in her eyes, and Pedro knew immediately that he was in danger.

"Ruthie! Ruthie!" he said firmly but softly, like you would speak to a frightened animal.

"Ruthie, it's me, Pedro. I'm not going to hurt you."

Ruthie continued to advance, causing Pedro to fall onto his back as she straddled his body, moving even closer to his face. Her eyes were still glowing.

"Ruthie! You're scaring me! Please stop!"

Pedro, now terrified, put his hands up as if to shield his face.

Ruthie blinked. She cocked her head sideways like a bird eyeing a worm. Then, like a television being turned off, the light in her eyes winked out, and she sat back on Pedro's legs and began to cry. Pedro sat frozen, unsure of what to do, but his instincts moved his hand out to pat Ruthie on her shoulder.

She was openly weeping now with full-chested sobs.

Pedro sat up and pulled Ruthie into his chest and patted her on the back.

"It's okay. Everything's going to be okay, Ruthie. Please don't cry." His hands still shook, but he comforted the creature who had just attacked him anyway. She was just a little girl, after all. Wasn't she? He wasn't so sure now.

He eventually got her to get up and go back to the blanket pile, gave her a juice box, and set about trying to clean up her face and hands. He went through the entire pack of wet wipes before she began to look a little better. The entire time, she just sat staring at him with those big blue eyes, her chest hitching now and then as she calmed down.

She ate two Pop-Tarts, dirtying her face again, and as soon as Pedro released her other hand from cleaning it off, she lay back down, burrowed under the blankets, and went back to sleep.

Pedro, still shaken, gathered up the trash, put it in the grocery bag he had brought, and quietly left the treehouse. He left two more juice boxes and some chips for her to eat later.

His head was filled with questions too big for him to answer. He didn't understand what happened. He reminded himself that she was just a scared little girl, but her inhuman face and those animal noises that had come out of her terrified him.

But then he thought, *What did he know?* He didn't have any little sisters. Maybe all little girls were capable of that when scared awake. He knew better, but had to make peace with that idea to keep from breaking down crying, or worse: being afraid of Ruthie. She was just a little girl. She had been through a lot.

When he arrived home, he went into the kitchen to find a big plate of atole and tamales that his mother had left for him. Both his parents worked at the chicken plant in Waynesboro, about 20 miles away. So, they left early every morning, but his mother always left him something scrumptious for breakfast. She had also packed him a lunch to take to the soccer clinic. The cooler was iced and sitting by the front door. He was riding with Dakota and then spending the night there with the other boys.

As he sat down at the breakfast bar to eat, he noticed a wrapped gift with his name on it sitting at the far side of the breakfast bar. He reached over and grabbed it. Inside, he found a new pair of shin guards and socks, a gift from his parents. He quickly finished his breakfast and hurried to put them on. He was growing fast and had outgrown his pads and socks from last year. He couldn't wait to show the guys. The Nike socks were black, and the pads were fluorescent green Nike pads. Even if his parents worked a lot and weren't home much of the time, they always seemed to know what he needed and when.

They were a tight-knit family. His brother was off at college with Dylan's brother, and that left just Pedro home alone much of the time. He missed his brother a lot. He'd know what to do about Ruthie, but Pedro had promised to tell no one, and he intended to keep that promise. Instead, he snapped a picture of his new socks and pads and texted it to his brother. His brother replied back almost immediately.

"Those are awesome, Pedro! Mom and Dad get those for you?"

Pedro replied back that they had and told him about his plans for the day. They exchanged a few more texts, and then Pedro grabbed his bag and went to wait outside for Dakota. Normally, they'd ride to the soccer fields on their bikes, but since Ruthie disappeared, their parents had gotten more protective and wanted to make sure they got there without any issues. They'd be really angry if they knew how often the boys had gone into the woods alone to the treehouse.

Even though his parents didn't speak much English, they knew what was going on with Ruthie. The posters that had been put up were in Spanish and English, as were the emails sent from the school. They had also gone to the candlelight vigil with the rest of the town. His mother worried incessantly about him, but his father, although worried, told his mother that Pedro was such a good wrestler and boxer that he could get away from anyone who tried to grab him, if needed. Pedro thought his father said that to bolster Pedro's courage more than anything, because he saw the worry in his father's eyes when they discussed it. They had no choice but to be gone, but that didn't mean they cared any less about him. He was well-loved.

CHAPTER NINE

They all arrived at the soccer field at roughly the same time. The boys ran out onto the field while the parents chatted with one another. The hot topic of the morning was that Joe Hamilton had been called back to the police station for more questioning. Of course he was going to be questioned, he was the stepfather, but many speculated as to why he'd been called back again last night and was still there.

This made Charlotte realize that she needed to make a decision about the memory stick with the files she had taken from Jalen's laptop. She had looked through it, but she didn't know what she was looking for. The police would know. She decided she would find a way to send it in anonymously.

Later that morning, news arrived of the death of Bill Snyder, a school bus driver. It was being said that his death was caused by an animal attack, possibly a bear or a stray dog. That didn't make sense to the parents because they had never seen a bear in this area. They were in north Georgia, but nothing like that had ever happened before.

"There are bears around here?" Charlotte asked Meg, looking alarmed.

"Never before this, I just don't believe it was a bear. I'm not buying that," Meg answered. "Now, a dog, yeah, there are some people who let their dogs run loose around here, but Bill was a large man. Hard to imagine a dog getting the better of him."

"I don't know, I've seen some of the bigger breeds get pretty aggressive," Charlotte replied and told them the story of an old man in their old neighborhood who had been killed by a couple of big dogs that had gotten away from their owner.

"Yeah, okay, makes sense, but it's just so weird, so many awful things happening at once here."

"Agreed. Too much for such a small town," Charlotte said, looking out at the field where the boys were doing drills, hoping she hadn't made a mistake moving to the little Georgia town.

Meg turned to Dylan's mother. "I'm glad Dylan decided to come tonight, Carolynn."

"Me too. He's been keeping himself cooped up alone in his room. He's really been anxious since Ruthie disappeared," Carolynn said, looking pensive. "He thinks he's seen her outside his window. He has nightmares at night and is very unsettled."

"Poor kid. It's scary stuff for all of us," Meg replied.

"Jalen hasn't been himself since this all started either," Charlotte chimed in, sympathetic to Carolynn's worry.

"Seems weird to be going on with life, going to soccer clinics, and having sleepovers, when someone's child is missing. But I guess we really need to so that our kids won't be paralyzed by fear, and we can keep them from being any more damaged from this than they already are."

"I agree, Charlotte," Meg replied.

"They are too young to have the weight of this on them," Carolynn added.

~ ~ ~

Ruthie hadn't been going out during the day. She'd just been so tired, but today was hot, and her body was restless. She made her way through the woods, passing the grave in which she had awoken. Anger filled her again and was quickly replaced by sadness. She didn't have a complete memory of what happened to her or how she ended up in the woods. She only had snippets, one of which was of her stepdad carrying her and crying. She remembered hearing him sob and say bad words. She didn't remember feeling pain, but she couldn't move. She felt his hands holding her too tightly and some kind of covering over her face. Prior to that, the memories were flashes of pain and violence, but always one face: her stepfather's.

She was jolted from her thoughts by the sound of children's laughter. She had unknowingly made her way to the park where children were playing. Ruthie hung back just inside the woodline where she could see them, but they couldn't see her. She saw her friends, and she longed to run to them and join in, but she knew she couldn't. She wasn't the same as them any longer. She didn't understand it. She just knew it to be true.

She saw Ava and Isabella, her best friends, swinging on the swings and laughing. She dropped to her knees with longing to be with them. She watched quietly as they jumped off the swings and went to their backpacks, which were laying on the ground by the swing set. Each girl took a Barbie doll from her bag and ran towards the playset near Ruthie, holding their dolls. Ruthie had dolls too, a whole bag full of them just like Ava and Isabella. She wished she had one with her.

As the girls came closer, Ruthie stood up to get a better view through the branches. Ava's head turned in her direction. She had heard her. Ruthie froze.

"Who is there?" Ava asked. She appeared as if she was looking right at Ruthie. Ruthie wanted to call out to her so badly that tears of frustration ran down her gaunt cheeks. Ava began to move closer, and Ruthie took a step back, breaking a stick.

"I know you're in there. I heard you. Is that you, Ruthie?" Ava asked, sounding hopeful.

Before she could stop herself, she quietly replied, "Yes."

Ava and Isabella rushed toward Ruthie but halted before they could embrace her. Ruthie's appearance stopped them in their tracks. Her hair was matted and dirty, with wide, bald patches on the top and one side. Her skin was pale and splotchy, and her eyes, dark and hollow, sank deeply into her cheeks. Her nightgown was smeared with dirt and stains, and her legs and arms were marred by purple bruises and deep, gaping cuts that exposed gray flesh.

The girls took in the sight, their faces reflecting their shock.

Ava, her voice barely above a whisper, asked, "What happened to you, Ruthie? Where have you been? Did you run away?" Her eyes widened as she scanned Ruthie's disheveled state.

"No," Ruthie responded, her gaze dropping to her dirty nightgown, feeling a wave of shame at being seen like this by her friends. "Someone hurt me."

Ava's eyes grew even wider, and Isabella interjected, "Who did this to you, Ruthie? Was it a bad man?"

"Yes, it was a bad man, Izzy."

"Why do you look like this?" Izzy asked, her nose crinkling as she became aware of the unpleasant odor emanating from Ruthie.

"I don't know," Ruthie said quietly, then added, "You can't tell anyone you saw me."

"Why not?" Ava asked, confused.

"Just promise me," Ruthie urged.

Both girls sensed that something was deeply wrong, both with the situation and with Ruthie herself. Reluctantly, they promised to keep her secret.

"I have some things to do before the grown-ups know I'm here," Ruthie told them. "They are secret."

"Are you going to catch the bad guy, Ruthie?" Ava asked her.

"Yes."

"And then will you tell the police so he can go to jail?"

"I don't know. I just know I have to do some things."

"Will you come see us again, Ruthie? We miss you," Izzy said, reaching out and grabbing Ruthie's hand in hers.

"I don't think so. I don't think I'll get to see anyone again."

Izzy's eyes welled up with tears and an understanding that she wouldn't see her friend ever again.

"Don't leave us, Ruthie. We miss you!" Ava cried out.

But Ruthie had already left them. She left them the day Joe Hamilton put her in that shallow grave. Ruthie began to cry too.

"You have to promise not to tell, or I won't be able to do what I'm supposed to do."

"We promise, Ruthie," the girls said in unison.

The three little girls stood holding hands, all of them crying, all of them with some unspoken knowledge that a bad thing had happened to Ruthie, and things would never be the same.

"Ava!!! Where are you?"

"That's my mom. We have to go, Ruthie. Are you sure you can't come see us again?"

Ruthie nodded her head.

"Okay then, here." Ava handed Ruthie the Barbie doll she'd been holding. "This is

Brooklyn. You know she's my favorite. You can have her, Ruthie. I'm going to miss you."

"Ava Marie McPherson!" Ava's mom's voice was louder this time.

Izzy and Ava turned and ran out of the woods and away from Ruthie to Ava's mother. Ruthie could hear her mother chiding the girls for going out of her sight.

She looked down at the doll Ava had given her and then clutched it to her chest.

The dark anger that lived inside Ruthie came roaring to life. She wanted to make Ava's mom stop yelling for her and let her stay there in the woods. She gritted her teeth, and her fists clenched with a burning hatred of grown-ups. Why couldn't she just leave them alone? The air seemed to swirl around her.

She drew her lips back into a snarl, wanting to rip Ava's mother into tiny pieces for taking her away, but she remembered she had other people she needed to see first. Maybe she would come back for Ava's mom later, but for now, she turned back to the woods, holding onto the doll her best friend had given her. It was the only piece of humanity she had left.

By the time Ruthie got back to the treehouse, she was exhausted. She lay down in her little pile of blankets with her doll and fell asleep. She needed rest. She had much left to do.

CHAPTER TEN

The boys burst through the door of Dakota's house, their laughter and animated chatter echoing throughout the entryway. Still buzzing with the adrenaline from their soccer clinic, they were a whirlwind of energy and excitement.

Dakota's mom, herding them with a mixture of practiced patience and good humor, guided them towards the basement. "Alright, boys, let's get you downstairs. The media room is all set up for you!"

The boys clambered down the stairs two at a time, their voices rising in a symphony of enthusiasm. At the bottom, the media room spread out before them like a treasure trove of entertainment: a large TV mounted on the wall, a gaming system with a pile of controllers, and a foosball table that promised hours of fun. There were also board games that the boys played on occasion as well as a bucket full of snacks on the coffee table. Everything set up for a night of fun for the boys.

Dakota's mom gave them a reassuring nod as she headed back upstairs to check on the pizzas. "I'll be back with your dinner in a bit. Remember, no snacks before the pizza arrives!"

The boys barely acknowledged her departure, their focus already on the TV. They flopped down onto the oversized couch, their earlier exhaustion forgotten in the face of the evening ahead.

Dakota grabbed a controller, instantly diving into a video game, while Pedro and Dylan challenged each other to a foosball match, their shouts and cheers mixing with the sounds of clacking rods and spinning players.

Dakota, sprawled comfortably with a controller in hand, looked around at his friends, a grin spreading across his face. "You think you can beat me at this level? I've been practicing!"

"Oh, it's on!" Jalen replied, raising an eyebrow challengingly.

The room was a whirlwind of movement and sound, with the boys' animated voices filling the space, punctuated by the occasional burst of laughter and the rhythmic clatter of foosball figures. As they lost themselves in the games and friendly rivalries, the anticipation of the pizza made the moment even sweeter.

The pizzas arrived about thirty minutes later, and the boys attacked them with the hungry fervor that only 12-year-old boys can produce. Meg just smiled and shook her head as she headed back upstairs.

All thoughts of the last few days' events were forgotten as the boys devoured pizza while balancing their video gaming controllers. There was no mention of Ruthie. For the moment, they were just boys having fun and enjoying their friends.

~ ~ ~

Christine and Meg sat down at the breakfast bar in the kitchen, opened a bottle of wine, and settled in to discuss the day's events.

Meg told Christine about the death of the bus driver and the mysterious circumstances surrounding it. Christine agreed that it was definitely not a bear.

The conversation moved on to Joe Hamilton and his repeat visit to the police station for more interviewing.

"Do you think he could have done something to Ruthie?" Meg asked Christine as she sipped her wine.

"I don't really know the man that well. He always seemed nice, but no one knows what goes on behind closed doors."

"That's true. I just hate to think that someone who has been around the kids could have done something to his own stepdaughter."

They continued talking as the cacophony of boy noises drifted up continuously from the floor below.

~ ~ ~

The backyard was quiet except for the faint hum of the pool's filter system and the soft rustling of leaves in the breeze. The sun was dipping low, casting long shadows across the yard.

Ruthie, with her tattered nightgown and pallid skin, shuffled across the worn wooden deck, her small feet barely making a sound. Her once vibrant eyes, now hollow and glazed, reflected the sinking sunlight as she moved.

Ruthie's eyes were locked on the sliding glass door that led into the house. She had watched the boys through the window, laughing and shouting as they played their video games. They hadn't come to the treehouse to see her. They hadn't even noticed her standing there, her small, waif-like figure pressed against the glass, yearning for attention. Her heart, if it still beat, would have been heavy with disappointment and sadness.

Her little fingers clenched into tiny, trembling fists, her nails cracking as she tried to hold back her growing frustration. She could hear their laughter, the clattering of game controllers, the occasional shout of triumph or defeat. It was as if their world was moving on without her, leaving her stranded in the loneliness of the evening.

Why hadn't they come to see her at the treehouse? She had forgotten that Pedro told her that morning they wouldn't be coming. Her thoughts were becoming harder to hold onto and remember.

The anger bubbled up, an uncontrollable surge that twisted her pale face into a grimace. Her hands, now sharper and more spectral, were trembling with the force of her emotion. She raised one hand, fingers stretched out like talons, and with a sudden, determined swipe, she struck the glass.

A sharp, splintering crack echoed through the yard as the glass shattered under the force of her touch. Shards flew outward, catching the last rays of the sun, before falling silently to the ground. Ruthie stared at the broken door, her breath coming in ragged, uneven bursts.

The boys' insides froze, their voices cut off abruptly as they turned in confusion and fear.

Pedro, with a look of wide-eyed horror, stood up and approached the door, peering out through the fragments of glass. Ruthie's eyes met his, and, for a moment, there was an eerie silence.

She felt a fleeting urge for violence as she saw the fear and surprise in his eyes, but it quickly dissolved into a deeper sadness.

With a final, resigned sigh, Ruthie turned and walked away from the door, her figure slowly blending into the growing darkness.

The boys watched her go, their game forgotten, as the night swallowed the broken glass and the haunting echoes of her frustration.

Inside, the boys remained silent, the only sounds now the distant buzz of the pool filter and the occasional crackle of glass underfoot. They knew they had witnessed something beyond their understanding, and the reality of Ruthie's presence lingered in the cold, fractured silence of the evening.

She was more than just a frightened little girl, and they knew that now.

Ten seconds later, Christine and Meg came charging down the stairs.

"What happened? Is everyone okay?" Christine asked urgently.

The boys stood frozen, their eyes wide and fixed on the shattered sliding glass door, their mouths hanging open. They couldn't reveal the truth—that a six-year-old girl had smashed the door with her bare hand.

Dakota finally broke the silence. "We don't know. We were just sitting here when the glass suddenly broke."

Meg moved cautiously toward the shards of glass. "Step back, guys. Be careful not to step on the glass." She examined the broken window and then turned to Christine. "I really don't know how this happened. You guys didn't throw a controller or anything, did you?"

The boys chorused in unison, "No!"

"Maybe I threw up a rock when I cut the grass the other day and caused a tiny crack that just decided to give way tonight? Regardless, you guys head upstairs to the living room. We'll relocate this party there. Gather your stuff and head up with Christine." Meg turned to Christine and said, "I'll cover this with plastic sheeting for the night."

Christine was guiding the boys upstairs when she noticed Dylan sitting on the floor, tears streaming down his face as he buried his head in his hands.

"It was Ruthie. She was there . . . We all saw her," he mumbled. Christine glanced at the other boys, who avoided her gaze or shrugged uncomfortably.

"Dylan, I'm sure it wasn't Ruthie," Christine said gently. "It was probably just a crack in the window."

"I saw her!" Dylan shot back, rising to his feet with clenched fists. "They saw her too, but they're too scared to tell you because we promised her we wouldn't."

Christine turned to Dakota, her eyes searching his face for answers. "What is he talking about, Dakota?"

Dakota glanced at Jalen and Pedro, his expression was a mix of hesitance and guilt. "I don't know, Mom. I didn't see anything," he said, his voice tinged with shame.

"I want to go home," Dylan sobbed.

"No problem, buddy. I'll call your mom now." Christine took Dylan upstairs with an arm around his shoulders as he continued to cry. The rest of the boys followed her up and began setting up in the living room.

While Christine and Dylan waited for his mother, the boys began creating a blanket fort in the living room facing the television. They got their gaming console set up and their snacks loaded into the space.

Once Dylan's mother had come and gone, Dakota's mothers retired to their bedroom to discuss the incident.

"What was that all about?" Dakota asked, glancing at the other two boys. "How did

Ruthie break the glass? What was she so angry about?"

Pedro shared his encounter with Ruthie that morning. He recounted how she had lunged at him like a wild animal after he accidentally touched her foot. The boys listened intently, their faces growing serious.

Finally, Jalen spoke up, his voice heavy with concern. "Do you think Ruthie might be . . . dangerous?"

"Dangerous how?" Dakota asked, looking puzzled. "She's just a little girl."

"Is she, though?" Pedro replied, his voice laced with unease. "We all know she's more than just a little girl."

"What do you mean?" Dakota asked, his fear beginning to surface.

Pedro took a deep breath. "We've all been thinking it. Ruthie isn't just a normal little girl. We found her buried, remember? Her skin is super pale, her eyes are sunken, and there's that strange smell. I think . . . I think she might be like a zombie."

"I don't know, Pedro. That seems pretty far-fetched," Jalen replied with his usual logic. "There's no such thing as zombies."

"Yeah, those are just in movies and books," Dakota added, shaking his head.

Pedro looked frustrated. "I don't know what she is, but 'zombie' is the closest word I could come up with. I mean, haven't you noticed all the strange things I have?"

Jalen paused, considering Pedro's words. "You're right. There's definitely something off about Ruthie. I can't say what she is, but she's not just an ordinary little girl."

Dakota, now visibly concerned, asked in a quiet voice, "Do you think she'll hurt us?"

The room fell into a tense silence.

Finally, Pedro spoke, his voice filled with uncertainty and fear. "I don't know."

As only children can, they soon turned their attention to the food and video games of the present, letting the topic of Ruthie go for the moment.

CHAPTER ELEVEN

The moon hung low in the sky, casting a ghostly pallor over the campsite as the shadows of towering trees danced in the flickering light of the dying campfire. Inside her tent, school nurse Glenda Dowry (or Miss Glenda, as the kids called her) lay on her cot, wrapped in the comfort of her favorite blanket. Her exhaustion was heavy, weighing her down into a deep sleep. She and her friends had hiked a fair distance that day and swam in the lake the remainder of the day. She took this trip with her friends yearly.

Outside, Ruthie, the once-vibrant six-year-old, now a haunting specter of her former self, moved with a chilling silence that belied her small stature. Her pale, bruised face was lit by the moonlight, eyes hollow but burning with a fierce, unsettling intensity and yellow glow. Scratches and cuts were etched into her delicate features, and her small hands, trembling slightly, clenched tightly as she approached the tent.

Miss Glenda's sleep was disturbed by the quiet rustling of the tent's fabric. She stirred, groggy and disoriented, but before she could fully awaken, Ruthie's small fingers had found their grip. With surprising strength, the undead girl grasped the nurse's ankles and began to drag her out of the tent, the fabric rustling loudly as it was pulled aside.

Miss Glenda's eyes flew open as she felt the sudden movement. Panic surged through her as she realized what was happening. Her heart pounded in her chest as she struggled to comprehend the situation.

"Ruthie?" she gasped, her voice barely a whisper, fraught with fear and disbelief.

The campfire, once a comforting source of warmth and light, now crackled menacingly, its flames casting eerie shadows on their faces.

Ruthie, with determined resolve, pulled Miss Glenda across the campsite, the back of her head dragging against the uneven ground. The nurse's pleas fell on deaf ears as Ruthie's silent fury drove her forward.

As they reached the edge of the firelight, Miss Glenda's eyes widened in terror. She tried to wriggle free, but Ruthie's grip was unyielding. The firelight danced on Ruthie's bruised skin, highlighting the depth of her anguish and the innocence that had been marred by suffering.

"Why . . . why are you doing this?" Miss Glenda's voice was shaky, her eyes filled with a blend of fear and guilt.

Ruthie's face, though still youthful, was set in a grim expression.

"Why didn't you help me?" Her voice was a chilling whisper that seemed to echo through the night. The question was both haunting and accusing, piercing through the stillness like a knife.

The nurse's breath hitched as she struggled, her feet almost brushing the edge of the fire. The flames flickered higher, casting a warm glow that seemed to taunt her with its cruel contrast to the cold, stark reality of Ruthie's suffering.

"I . . . I didn't know . . ." Miss Glenda stammered, her voice breaking as tears welled up in her eyes. "I was trying . . . I was overwhelmed . . ."

But Ruthie's expression remained unchanged, her gaze fixed on the terrified woman with an intensity that spoke of pain and broken trust. The flames crackled louder, as if in response to the tension mounting between them. Miss Glenda had seen the bruises. Miss Glenda had known something was not right with little Ruthie.

Ruthie's grip tightened, and the heat of the fire grew more intense.

"I needed you," she said softly, the words carrying the weight of a child's unfulfilled need for protection and care.

Miss Glenda's face was illuminated by the fire's light, the terror etched into every line as she met Ruthie's gaze. The night seemed to hold its breath, the crackle of the fire the only sound as the two figures were locked in a moment of raw, painful confrontation.

Ruthie continued moving towards the campfire. Miss Glenda was too terrified to call out for help. Her voice, as well as her breath, had left her in the midst of her terror. Ruthie pulled her feet into the fire, seemingly unaffected by it herself.

The heat sent searing pain through Miss Glenda's body. She felt her skin burn. Then, Ruthie pulled her deeper into the dancing orange flames, and she felt the heat on the backs of her thighs and buttocks. Her skin began to bubble.

She found her voice at the same moment that Ruthie released her grip and let out a bloodcurdling shriek. Her clothes were now on fire, and she thrashed desperately about, trying to push herself away from the fire. As she scrambled on burning hands to remove herself, she saw a shadow fall across her body.

Ruthie brought the large rock down before she could take a breath to scream again, smashing her face into a bloody, unrecognizable pulp that glistened in the firelight. It was nothing more than a shiny mass of blood and bone. She fell silent, and Ruthie pushed the rest of her limp body into the fire. The campsite was filled with the vile smell of burning flesh. Her friends burst out of their tents, but it was too late. There was nothing that could be done to save Miss Glenda any more than there was anything that could be done to save Ruthie.

Her friends saw no one but Miss Glenda there in the glow of the campfire, Ruthie having disappeared into the darkness.

CHAPTER TWELVE

Miles away, the boys were done playing games and settled into their sleeping bags. They all lay silently with their thoughts until Jalen spoke up.

"I don't know if we can still help Ruthie, guys."

The silence returned and stretched as the boys considered all that had happened.

"But how will she take care of herself? How will she eat?" asked Pedro.

"I don't know if it's safe for us, Pedro." Jalen sat up in his sleeping bag and turned to face Pedro to his left. "Something is wrong with her. What if she *is* a zombie? Will she eat us or hurt us in some way? You already said she got all crazy with you."

"I think I startled her." Pedro sat up now as well. "We promised," he said as he began to pick at a thread on the green sleeping bag he was nestled into.

"What do you think, Dakota?" Jalen asked, looking at the still reclining Dakota.

Dakota seemed to mull their words over and finally answered. "Maybe we just leave her food under the treehouse?"

"Who is going to help her bust her stepfather if we don't?" Pedro's response was almost pleading with the other boys.

What Pedro didn't know was that Jalen's mother had packaged up the thumb drive and would be dropping it in the mail that morning. Help may not be too far away.

After a prolonged discussion that lasted about an hour, the boys decided that zombies weren't real and, even if they were, they can't talk. Ruthie can talk. If zombies were even real, she wasn't one. However, they did decide they would only go together to see Ruthie in case she got upset again.

~ ~ ~

Meanwhile, an almost inconsolable Dylan was finally settled down and in bed with his parents, a place he hadn't been in years. He was sure Ruthie would know he'd told them about her and come for him. He could not be convinced otherwise. His parents finally offered to let him sleep with them that night, and he quickly took them up on that offer.

At around 3:30 a.m., Dylan was jolted awake by the creak of his parents' door. Paralyzed by fear, he lay still, eyes locked on the dark void of the doorway. The house was silent except for the steady hum of the ceiling fan and the air conditioner. The door creaked slightly again, sending Dylan's heart racing. Though the doorway was cloaked in pitch black, he was certain he had heard something.

Suddenly, two glowing eyes emerged from the darkness, blinking open before him. It was Ruthie. The yellow orbs flickered on and off as she began to inch closer to the bed. Dylan felt the icy grip of terror; he was unable to move or make a sound, his breaths coming in shallow, panicked gasps. As the eyes drew nearer, Dylan's fear intensified.

Ruthie had come for him, just as she had promised. A whimper escaped Dylan's lips, his hand clutching the blanket tightly. The eyes hovered at the edge of the bed before disappearing. At that moment, Dylan found his voice and screamed as loud as he could.

His mother sprang up, reaching for the bedside lamp and switching it on just as the shadowy figure lunged onto the bed.

It was Gracie, the cat. She regarded Dylan with an indifferent glance before starting to lick her paw. Dylan's mother quickly pulled him into a comforting embrace while his father, also awakened by the commotion, sat up and looked around.

"It's just Gracie, Dylan." She stroked his head and cast a worried look at his father. Dylan sobbed and shook, unable to calm himself.

His father went to get him a drink and nodded at his mother when he returned with liquid Benadryl and a glass of water. They weren't ones to drug their children, but an earlier call to the pediatrician's after-hours number had assured them that, if they couldn't calm him down, the Benadryl would help.

Dylan took the Benadryl and a sip of water, then lay down against his mother and, within ten minutes, drifted off to sleep.

Ruthie hadn't come for him that night, but he knew she would eventually.

He was certain.

~ ~ ~

The next morning, Dakota, Jalen, and Pedro slept in.

As they were in the living room, which was connected to the kitchen in a large open concept, they could hear conversations being had in the kitchen.

Jalen woke up before the other boys and heard one of Dakota's mothers talking to his own mom on the phone about Joseph Hamilton. It seemed the police department had a leak, and it had somehow reached Charlotte.

Joseph Hamilton was in for another day of questioning at the police station. He had been there the day before as well. It had somehow gotten out that the police were digging into Joseph's past and discovered another incident with a child in his care.

Jalen couldn't hear both sides of the conversation, but knew this was important stuff. He nudged his friends awake and motioned for them to listen.

"He had another family almost 20 years ago. He and his first wife had a daughter who died in a house fire." Christine was relaying information to Meg as Charlotte spoke. "I guess the police are asking questions now about that child and what happened to her."

Just then, Christine looked up and saw the boys were awake and lowered her voice. They could only hear mumbles from that point on. When she hung up, she and Meg spoke in hushed tones. Jalen caught the word "allegations" and the word "abuse."

The boys looked at each other wide-eyed. Jalen knew he had to dig into this the minute he could lay his hands on his laptop.

"I see you sleepy heads are up!" Christine went into the living room and plopped down on the couch above the boys. "You guys want some breakfast? There are all types of cereal, Pop-Tarts, and donuts in the kitchen. You can have whatever you like, but just make sure to clean up after yourselves."

The boys immediately began to hop up and make their way to the kitchen.

"And clean up . . . right, Dakota?" she asked, giving Dakota a look, which meant she was serious.

"Okaaaay, Mom. Geez!" Dakota replied, embarrassed as any 12-year-old would be by his mother speaking to him in front of his friends, much less chiding him.

"Just making sure. We will let you boys have the living room to play your games for a while after you eat before we take everyone home. Momma Meg and I will be out on the patio if you need us."

"Okay," Dakota replied, already dismissing his mother and tearing open a box of donuts.

The boys all fixed cereal, grabbed three or four donuts each to go with the cereal, and climbed up onto the lifted chairs at the kitchen bar.

"He had another family?" Dakota began the conversation about what they had overheard earlier.

"I'm going to do some research on my laptop later today," Jalen replied while shoving cereal into his mouth.

"What do you think that means?" Pedro looked at Jalen and then at Dakota.

"You know what it means. He had another kid and probably hurt her too. I wonder if Ruthie knows about her?" Jalen said, still shoveling cereal into his mouth and swallowing huge mouthfuls, as only 12-year-old boys can.

"Dang, Jalen. How can you even talk with that face full of cereal?" Pedro laughed.

"Shut it, Pedro. I'm starving. If I want to play football this year, I have to bulk up. That's what Coach Watson said. Anyway, what do you think? Does Ruthie know?"

"Nah, she's little. She's only six years old. I doubt they told her anything about that kind of stuff. She won't know anything," Pedro said assuredly. "What are you going to look up, Jalen?"

"Whatever I can find on Mr. Hamilton, the house fire, and his family."

"Are we going to see Ruthie today?" Dakota had finished his third donut, and his mouth and cheeks were covered in chocolate.

"Do you think we should? "Jalen was downing another donut.

"Put a couple donuts and some cereal in bags, and I will take it to her after I get dropped off home. My parents are at work," Pedro volunteered.

"I thought we agreed no one would go alone?" Jalen stopped stuffing his face to look at Pedro with a serious expression.

"How can we all get out today? She needs food," Pedro replied.

~ ~ ~

Meanwhile, Ruthie was starting to stir in the treehouse. There was a heavy feeling in her limbs, and her teeth felt strange. She rubbed her fingers across her top row of teeth. She pulled her hand away, and a tooth came with it. Astonished, she stared at it. Her tooth had fallen out! Although she wasn't sure how she knew, she knew the tooth fairy wouldn't come.

She felt anger rising within her. She wanted to lash out at something, anything. This urge was becoming stronger each day. She was losing focus on what she knew she was there to do.

She looked at her leg where the fire had burned her the night before and saw that the flesh was black and jaggedly torn open in spots. There was no blood nor scabs, just the meaty flesh of her leg exposed. It didn't hurt, but it should have. Her body felt numb to pain.

She wondered if the boys would visit her today. She hoped they would. Ruthie began to feel tired again. Her energy was waning quickly. She curled up in the sleeping bags and fell back to sleep.

Flies began to swirl around her little body, and other insects had begun to investigate her as well.

Her time was running out.

CHAPTER THIRTEEN

Around noon, Dakota's mothers drove each boy to his home. The boys still had not decided how to visit Ruthie, but Pedro took the bag of donuts and cereal with him, just in case. He was determined to get it to her whether the other boys went with him or not. Although the events of the morning before had frightened him, his concern for Ruthie outweighed his fear.

Jalen went home, grabbed his laptop, and went straight to his room. He had digging to do. He spent the day reviewing the footage he had gotten from the Hamiltons' cameras but, being only 12, he didn't see anything that stood out as suspicious to him.

He was still unaware that his mother had mailed a copy to the police. He was unaware she had even seen it. When she knocked on his door and asked to speak with him, he had no idea what it was about.

"Jalen, listen, you're a good boy, and I know this stuff with Ruthie has touched your heart, but you have to promise me you won't get involved." Jalen started to reply, but she cut him off. "I know you hacked his cameras and downloaded the footage, Jalen. I know you meant well, but this is a dangerous situation, and the police will handle it. You are a very smart and observant young man, but this is truly an adult matter that you need to let the police deal with. I promise they are working on it."

Jalen's face paled. How did she know? He was glad he'd shut his laptop when she entered the room or she'd have seen what he had been looking at on his screen.

"I want you to delete the footage off your laptop. Now."

"Yes, ma'am." Jalen immediately opened his laptop and deleted the file containing the footage.

"Thank you. Again, honey, I love you, and I know you were just trying to help, but like I said, this is a dangerous situation. You're grown enough to know that there isn't much hope that they will find Ruthie alive at this point and that the police probably have the same suspicions as you do about Joe Hamilton. If there is the possibility that he did something bad to his own stepdaughter, what do you think he'd do to you if he found out you were snooping?"

Those words sent a cold chill down Jalen's spine. He wanted to tell his mother what he knew. He wanted to tell her about Ruthie, but he couldn't. A promise was a promise.

"I couldn't stand it if something were to happen to you, Jay." Charlotte's eyes glassed over, and she reached out and patted her son on the knee. He was too old to pull him onto her lap for a hug, even though that's exactly what she wanted to do at that moment. "You understand?"

"I do. I'm sorry, Mom. Like you said, I just wanted to help."

Charlotte nodded at him, patted his knee again, and got up to leave.

"What do you have planned for the rest of the day?" she asked.

"I'm going to play on my laptop and then maybe go to Pedro's house later, if that's okay."

"That's fine with me, sweetheart. You need to go and enjoy being a kid. This stuff with Ruthie isn't for you to worry about, okay?"

"Okay, Mom."

"Love you, buddy."

"Love you too, Mom."

Charlotte left the room and Jalen sat staring at his laptop screen for a few minutes. He logged onto Discord and found Pedro there.

"Hey man, my mom found the video from Mr. Hamilton's house."

"Oh shit!"

"Yeah, she made me delete it all."

"Oh damn. What are we going to do?" Pedro asked him.

"I don't know. I still haven't dug into Mr. Hamilton online yet. Let me do that, and we'll see what I find. I told my mom I was going to go to your house later today. We can go see Ruthie."

"Okay, cool. Text me when you are on the way. I have to do some chores before my parents get home, so I'll get booking on those right now."

"Later."

"Later," replied Jalen.

~ ~ ~

Midafternoon, Jalen met Pedro at his house, and they started off towards the park. As they approached the entrance, they saw a dead squirrel in the gutter. It had obviously been there for days. They got within six feet of the squirrel, and the smell hit their noses. They made faces and pinched their noses closed.

Both stopped walking at almost the exact same time and turned to look at each other. The realization struck them almost simultaneously. That was the same odor they had smelled in the treehouse. That was what Ruthie smelled like—death. Neither spoke out loud, but the revelation impacted each boy tremendously, and the confusion they felt was deep.

Why did Ruthie smell like a dead animal? They both went through the possibilities in their heads. Maybe she picked up a dead animal? No, that was ridiculous. Why would she do that?

Finally, Pedro spoke. "What does that mean, Jalen?"

"I don't know, Pedro. It's really weird. Maybe she's just extremely dirty."

"I gave her wet wipes to clean with."

"That doesn't mean she used them."

"Maybe not. I don't know. But that smell . . ."

"I know. There's really nothing as gross as that, man. Why does a little girl smell like that?"

They continued on in silence, both lost in their own thoughts. They made their way through the park and into the woods. Neither spoke. They passed the grave from which they had saved Ruthie, and a chill ran up their spines. That hole was beginning to take on a new meaning to the boys, but precisely what that was, neither of them knew. With the events of last night and this revelation, the boys were confused and unsure. They were unsure about the entire situation, but ideas were forming in both boys' heads about what Ruthie might be.

When you are young, before the world has interrupted your mind with science and reality, it's easier to believe the unbelievable. Your thoughts haven't been polluted with the rules of adult reality yet, and all things are still possible.

As they approached the treehouse, the smell they had just experienced passing the squirrel began to invade their noses. They glanced quickly at one another and approached the rope to the treehouse with new caution, obtained not only by the events last night, but through the realization of what Ruthie smelled like.

Pedro climbed the rope first. He slowly made his way up and cautiously poked his head through the entrance. He immediately saw Ruthie. She was sitting straight up on the sleeping bags and staring at him with her faded blue eyes.

Did eyes fade? If it was possible, her eyes appeared more sunken than before. Deep, purplish black bags hung underneath. The rest of her skin was almost porcelain in color.

He noticed how skinny her little neck seemed now and, to his dismay, the bits of skin that had begun flaking off on her face and neck. They were like scabs when you picked them too soon, flaky on top and wet underneath. Her skin seemed to be oozing and flaking at the same time. The sight took Pedro aback.

Also, more of her hair had fallen out and lay in a blonde mass on her pillow. Her frame was wasted, and her nightshirt hung more loosely around her.

She smiled at Pedro, and he gasped. She was missing teeth in the front of her mouth, and her gums were almost gray. The smell was nearly overpowering, and Pedro had to swallow hard to keep from gagging.

What was happening?

She uncovered her legs to get up and greet the boys. She had an excited look on her haggard face. As she threw the sleeping bag back, a new and much worse smell hit Pedro full in the face. It was that of rotten cooked meat.

Jalen was attempting to enter the treehouse and had to push the stunned Pedro out of the way to gain entrance. He entered just in time to see the horror that Ruthie had uncovered.

Her legs looked burned. The skin was brown and dark black in places, it looked like burned chicken. There were gaping wounds on the side of her left calf. They hung open, exposing the tendons underneath. Jalen swore he saw a glimmer of bone as well. It looked like meat that had been cooked too long, how it swelled and then cracked open.

With the recent revelation about the odor they smelled from Ruthie and the sight before them, both boys stood frozen to the spot. Neither was able to take their eyes off the spectacle before them and reconcile it with the little girl they had rescued a few days ago. Speaking or moving was not possible.

Pedro was the first to speak as Ruthie began limping towards him, arms outstretched.

"Ruthie! What happened to your legs?" He embraced her, trying not to recoil.

In her whispery voice, Ruthie answered, "I'm not sure. I think it happened last night."

Jalen added, "Ruthie, you're burnt! How do you not know what happened? Did you leave the treehouse last night?"

"Yes, but my head is jumbled." Ruthie let go of Pedro and looked down at the ground.

"Do you leave the treehouse every night?"

"Sometimes. I just go. I have to go," she replied to Jalen, not looking up.

"What do you mean you have to go? Go where?" Jalen was shocked to learn little Ruthie had been going out at night, alone.

"I don't know. I . . . I have things to do." Her voice was barely a whisper.

"What things?" Jalen pushed her for an answer.

"I'm not supposed to tell." Ruthie was getting upset. Her faded blue eyes filled with tears as she spoke.

Noticing this, Pedro stepped in.

"Ruthie, we are your friends, you can tell us. We are trying to protect you and help you."

Ruthie continued to stare down at her feet. She clasped her hands behind her back and began to twist her body from left to right, as children do when they do not want to answer a question.

"She told me not to tell anyone."

"Who told you that? "Jalen asked.

"Laura."

Jalen and Pedro exchanged looks.

"She visits me when you aren't here. She was hurt too."

"She visits you? Can we meet her, Ruthie? Maybe we can help her too." Pedro took a small step towards Ruthie, and despite his nose's desire to recoil, placed a hand on her tiny shoulder.

"Maybe. I mean, I don't think you can see her. She told me that no one can see her but me."

"What do you mean, 'see her'? Like with our eyes?"

Ruthie nodded her head.

"She told me you are trying to help, but that you are in danger and could get hurt."

Jalen swallowed audibly before asking, "Hurt? How?"

"By him . . . my stepdad."

"He can't hurt us, Ruthie. He doesn't know we are helping you."

"Laura said he knows you took something from his house."

Jalen was taken aback. How could Mr. Hamilton know they took the video from his house?

"How do you know that, Ruthie?"

"Laura told me. She said whatever it was, the police have it now, and he's really angry."

Jalen's stomach fell and he felt instant panic at the thought that Joe Hamilton knew they took the footage. He also simultaneously realized that his mother must have sent the footage to the police. That's why she was so insistent he delete the videos from his laptop. She had unwittingly put him and the other boys in danger.

"How does Laura know that?" It was Pedro's turn to ask questions. He knew, like Jalen, that she had to be referring to the footage that Jalen had taken from Mr. Hamilton's house on the night of the candlelight vigil.

"I'm not sure. She is around my stepdad a lot. She stays around his house most of the time. She said he hurt her too, and she will stay with him to remind him until he dies."

None of that made sense to Jalen and Pedro.

"I don't understand. Maybe we can talk to Laura."

"I told you. You can't see her, only I can see her."

Pedro and Jalen didn't know what to think. Pedro gave Ruthie the food they had brought her, and she sat down and hungrily began to rip open the bags of donuts and cereal. While she did that, Jalen and Pedro walked to the other side of the treehouse to talk.

"I'm so confused," Pedro whispered to Jalen.

"Me too, but if Mr. Hamilton really does know we took the footage, we have to warn the guys."

Branches snapped below the treehouse. Pedro and Jalen both jumped. Ruthie's news had put them on edge. Suddenly, the treehouse didn't feel safe any longer.

Jalen poked his head out the window of the treehouse and saw no one. It must have been a squirrel or a deer.

"Listen, Ruthie. We have to go now. Don't leave this treehouse. It's not safe. Please tell Laura we'd really like to talk to her, okay?"

"I will. Thank you for the food."

At that moment, Pedro noticed a doll laying in the pile of sleeping bags.

"Ruthie, where did you get that doll?"

Ruthie was busy nibbling on a donut. She looked up with wide eyes.

"Promise you won't get mad?"

"No, I'm not gonna get mad, but where did you get it?"

Ruthie stopped eating and looked down. "I got it from my friend. She gave it to me." She reached over and grabbed the doll then, clutching it to her chest and dropping the donut bag.

"Ruthie! Did you go visit a friend? What if someone saw you?" Jalen exclaimed a bit louder and harsher than he intended.

Ruthie's pale eyes filled with tears.

"I just saw them in the park. I couldn't help it. I miss my friends and my dollies."

A single tear ran down her cheek, and she crumpled into herself, sobbing.

"I miss my mommy. I miss everyone." She was crying now. Pedro ran to her side and knelt down on the sleeping bag next to her. He took her into his arms and hugged her.

He looked back at Jalen and said, "Just leave it, Jalen."

Jalen nodded. He was reminded that Ruthie was just a little girl and how scared she must be. He thought about if one of his sisters was in Ruthie's shoes, and he immediately regretted raising his voice.

"I'm sorry, Ruthie. I didn't mean to yell at you. I'm just worried for you. Please don't cry. Keep your doll. I know it's important to you."

Ruthie nodded her head and buried her face in Pedro's chest. Bald patches on the back of her head were even more evident from that angle. Jalen flinched.

"It's not fair! It's not fair that I can't play with my dollies or my friends!" She raised her hoarse voice as much as she could.

The air around them chilled suddenly. Pedro felt Ruthie begin to tremble, almost vibrate, in his arms. He released her and stood up, backing away. The treehouse began to darken, and when Ruthie looked up, her eyes were glowing. Her lips drew back from her teeth in a snarl.

Then, she was standing, fists clenched, and boomed in a voice louder than they'd heard her ever use before, "HE HURT ME! WHY DIDN'T ANYONE HELP ME? THEY SHOULD HAVE HELPED ME! THE GROWN-UPS SHOULD HAVE HELPED ME!"

The treehouse shook, and both Pedro and Jalen scrambled towards the hole in the center of the treehouse floor, shocked and terrified. They practically jumped through the hole, landing in a pile on the ground beneath the treehouse. The wind was blowing, and the clouds turned darker by the second. They could hear items blowing around in the treehouse, banging against the walls. Paper flew from the windows and furniture thudded above.

If they could have seen Ruthie, they would have seen her eyes aglow, her hair blowing around her haggard face, and her little, rotting fists clenched as chaos blew around her.

The boys began to run as fast as they could away from the treehouse. They didn't stop running until they reached the park, both panting for breath and pale with fear. They only stopped to catch their breath and then ran all the way back to Pedro's house.

CHAPTER FOURTEEN

Back at the treehouse, things had calmed. Ruthie's anger left quickly, and she was left with only confusion and sadness. She felt a familiar presence behind her.

Laura was a fuzzy image, much like when she first woke up in the morning and had blurry eyes. She had come to Ruthie the day after the boys found her. At first, she was afraid of Laura. She had materialized before Ruthie's eyes one night but was never a completely clear image. Then, she saw the same bruises around Laura's neck that she had on hers, and Laura told her that her stepfather had hurt her too. He had been her father a long time ago. She had a different mommy than Ruthie. Since then, Laura had visited her most nights and sometimes gone along with her as she visited the adults who should have saved her, but did nothing. Laura had told her she was proud of her and wished that she could do the same. Ruthie wished she could visit the people who let Laura down, but she knew she didn't have enough time left.

Laura was older than Ruthie. She told her she was 14 when she died and that she was now a ghost. Ruthie wasn't sure she understood what a ghost was, but Laura told her that no one else could see her except Ruthie. Ruthie felt better having a friend nearby. It made her nights less lonely. During the day and the rest of the nights that she wasn't with Ruthie, Laura was at Ruthie's home. She told her she had been there the whole time Ruthie was there and had seen all that had happened. She understood, and she knew that their father must be made to pay for what he had done to them. Laura had been enacting her own justice by invading her father's thoughts and being a presence that he could feel. She wished she could strike out at him, but the most she could do was unsettle him with blinking lights and thumps in the night. Ruthie had never seen any blinking lights or heard thumps in the night. Laura told her she only did it around their father because she didn't want to scare anyone else.

"There is only one more person to visit, Ruthie," Laura said to her. Her mouth didn't move, but Ruthie could still hear her somehow.

"Two," Ruthie corrected her. "I want to see my mommy and ask her why she let him hurt me."

"Two," Laura agreed. She smiled at Ruthie and asked her if she wanted to play dolls, but Ruthie was too tired and she needed to save her energy for what was to come. She asked Laura if she would stay with her while she slept, and Laura agreed.

Ruthie crawled into one of the sleeping bags on the floor, pulled her doll into a cuddle, and was soon asleep.

~ ~ ~

Twenty years earlier, Laura had been a pretty 14-year-old girl with long golden hair, big blue eyes, and a dimple on her left cheek. She played softball, did cheerleading, and had many friends. Her mother and father came to every game, they went on vacations every summer, and lived in a nice home. From all appearances, she had a happy life, but what she actually had was a dark secret that she'd been hiding since she was a little girl.

They lived in a small southern Georgia town. Bruises had been seen, but people just didn't meddle in other family's business, and her father often mentioned to anyone who would listen, how "clumsy" she was. He said she was always falling down or bumping into things at home. Playing softball and cheerleading were also good excuses for bruises.

Her mother had the same bruises and the same secrets. People were even less likely to get involved when an adult showed up with a black eye or bruises on her arms.

"These two are like living with circus clowns, falling down and bumping into things. Clumsiest pair you've ever seen," her father would often say. Janice, her mother, just smiled and went along with him, never showing her fear or pain. Laura learned to do the same.

There were other things happening though, darker things than physical abuse, and when Laura became older, more mature, she realized that what had been happening to her was wrong. Fathers didn't do those things to daughters. She confided in her best friend one tearful night. She was confused and had been sick in the mornings for three days. The two of them shoplifted a pregnancy test from CVS that night, and the terrible news was revealed. Laura was pregnant.

One week later, she was dead in a house fire. Her best friend, Lindsey, had never recovered from the trauma of it all. She felt responsible because, even though the fire was ruled accidental, she knew after she told her own mother about the situation with Laura, that her mother had gone to the authorities. Laura told her a sheriff's deputy had visited the house. She told her she was being taken downtown the next day to speak with someone. That day never came. Laura was dead that night.

The fire had been ruled accidental, and the report was never followed up, but Lindsey knew. She knew that Joe Hamilton had killed her best friend because he had impregnated her, and the police were about to find out. Lindsey's mother tried to get the authorities to look deeper into the fire, to listen to her when she told them what was going on in that home. They had made their ruling and told her there was no longer anyone to prove or disprove the claims because Laura was dead.

Lindsey never forgot Laura. She had been keeping track of Joe Hamilton since that day. When she read about the disappearance of Ruthie in an online news article, she knew she had to act.

CHAPTER FIFTEEN

Joe Hamilton walked into his home, tossed his suit coat on the table, and made his way to the refrigerator to get a beer. He was a 55-year-old man who looked like every school principal had ever looked. He was about six feet tall, fit, with an ever-so-slight beer belly showing over his suit pants, beginning to press against the buttons of his neatly pressed shirts. He had dark, thinning hair that he styled with a little bit of a comb-over and pomade. His face always carried a neutral, yet harmless, expression, and when speaking to adults, he sounded like a well-polished politician.

He didn't have much day-to-day interaction with the students, as that was handled by his vice principal, but he did make appearances in the hall on occasion, popped his head into classrooms, and went to all the pep rallies. The adults saw him as a good, solid character who cared about his students and his community. He never missed an opportunity to glad-hand with parents and other townspeople. He was a pillar of the community.

It had been a long day at the police station, and he faced another one the next day. All the lights were off in the house and the bedroom door closed. He assumed Julia was sleeping. That's what she did most of the time now since Ruthie had been gone. The press had spoken to her numerous times, and the search teams kept her updated as well. They had dragged a nearby lake yesterday. Julia spent the day wringing her hands, sitting at the table with her phone right next to her. When the call finally came that they had found nothing, she heaved a sigh of relief, burst into tears, and immediately headed back to the bedroom.

As he cracked open his beer, he noticed that damn light in the dining room blinking again. He would have to have an electrician come out again eventually. It had been doing that for years, but every time he tried to have someone check, it wouldn't reproduce the blinking. It seemed to only happen when he was alone in the room. Whatever, he had much more to worry about right now than a blinking light.

ZAP! The toaster cord popped as he passed it. No time for that either. He made his way into the living room and threw himself into his recliner. He didn't know for sure what people in town thought about his frequent trips to the police station. He knew they knew about them. Everyone knew everything that went on in this town.

I should have picked a larger city in which to live, he thought to himself.

His wife was quiet and did not understand why the police were interviewing him so much. He explained to her that it was standard procedure to look at the stepfather. Thus far, they hadn't pushed him too hard, but he could feel it coming. He wasn't sure how strongly they felt about him as a suspect. He had been thrown for a loop today when they produced video from his home. Although he felt like he had sufficiently explained it away, he was simmering with rage at the fact that they even had it. Those damn boys. He knew it was Pedro, Jalen, Dakota, and Dylan who had gotten it, moreso Jalen. He was well aware of his hacking skills and should have moved him off his property the moment he saw them sitting there with the laptop. He would deal with them when it was safe to do so. He had a long memory and patience. Interfering little shits.

He launched himself up out of the recliner and went into the kitchen to grab a pack of peanut butter crackers. He hadn't eaten all day, and Julia wasn't going to cook for him. She barely ate herself, or cleaned the house, or attended to her husband in any way since this started. As he made his way back to the living room, he stumbled on a discarded doll that belonged to Ruthie. He stared at it for a moment before stepping on the doll's head and heading back into the living room. He was weary of all of this and was already planning to pick up sticks and move, get a fresh start (again) when this was all over. Julia may or may not be willing to move. Either way, he was going.

The lamp in the living room flickered. Joe ignored it, grabbed the remote to turn on the TV, and eventually dozed off in his recliner.

~ ~ ~

Jalen, Pedro, and Dakota were at their homes, on their computers in a Discord chat discussing the events of the day. Jalen and Pedro told Dakota all that had happened, including the warning from the supposed ghost, Laura. She had to be real because how else would she or Ruthie know about what Mr. Hamiton did or did not know?

As they discussed all that occurred today, Dakota brought up the idea of arming themselves. The boys all agreed that they should keep their pocket knives in their pockets at all times and their baseball bats by their beds, just in case.

What they couldn't decide was what to do about Ruthie. She had really scared Jalen and Pedro, but Pedro kept pointing out that she had not hurt them.

"She threw a fit, basically," Pedro said, trying to continue to convince the boys not to abandon her or their promise to help.

"Yeah, she threw a fit that also threw all the shit around the treehouse and made the wind blow. I don't know what she is for sure, Pedro, but she could hurt us."

"But she didn't, and she wouldn't. You saw her. She was tired and upset. I don't know what she is either, but I know we promised to help her," Pedro insisted as he continued his campaign to support Ruthie.

"I think she's some kind of monster we haven't heard of before," Dakota chimed in with his two cents.

"Monster? She's a little girl!" Pedro questioned Dakota's description.

"Come on, Pedro! She's more than a little girl. She really is kind of a zombie."

"Not any zombie I've seen in a movie," Pedro countered.

"Yeah, movies. How do we know what zombies *really* look like, Pedro? We don't. Maybe she is something in between, but she's not just a regular little girl," Dakota pressed.

"Okay. So, we agree she's not human. It doesn't really matter what she is. It matters whether or not she'll hurt us," Jalen interjected.

Dylan entered the Discord chat just as Jalen was speaking and caught what he said about Ruthie.

"She can and will hurt you."

"Hey, Dylan! Where you been?" Dakota felt guilty for not backing Dylan the night before.

"She can and will hurt you." Dylan ignored Dakota and repeated what he had said.

"Why do you say that, Dylan? You haven't seen her since that first day," Pedro snapped.

Dylan began to tell the boys about Ruthie's "visits" to his house. When he was finished, no one in the group spoke.

"But AGAIN, she didn't HURT you or us," Pedro piped in, reiterating his original point with a slightly agitated tone.

"Who's to say she won't though, Pedro?" Dylan's voice was shaky from the fear the retelling of events had caused him.

"Dude, you've been scared of her from day one. You don't get a say in this!" Pedro retorted, his irritation with Dylan's fear apparent in his voice. "You're scared of your own freaking shadow, Dylan. You run off to mommy every time something a little weird happens. So, again, you don't get a say in this." Pedro felt defensive of Ruthie. Had they all forgotten what happened to her or why she was even in their treehouse to start with?

"Heyyyy, chill," Dakota broke into the conversation. "Dylan, no worries, man. We hear you. That was not cool, Pedro. Calm down."

Pedro just sat silently for a moment and then said, "I'm sorry, Dylan. I didn't mean it. Ruthie has been through a lot, and she came to US for help. What kind of men would we be if we didn't help her? My dad always tells me that the measure of a man is determined by his actions."

"But we aren't men, Pedro," Dakota responded to Pedro's assertion.

"Man, we are 12, almost 13."

"Yes, we are, but even if we aren't, Pedro's right. We made a promise." Jalen had made up his mind.

"Exactly." Pedro knew Jalen agreed with him.

"Okay, but I'm bringing my knife." Dakota finally gave in.

Jalen hopped out of Discord and began his online investigation into Joe Hamilton's other daughter. While doing so, he came upon the name Lindsey Derringer. She was Laura's best friend at the time of her death. She had created a website in remembrance of Laura and made some not-so-subtle statements about how the case hadn't been investigated thoroughly. It was clear she believed that Laura had been murdered.

He wondered if he should reach out to her. His only hesitation was his age. Would she listen to a kid? He decided to give it a shot. He found her on Facebook and sent her a message. A few minutes later she replied.

"Hi Jalen, thanks for reaching out. I am aware of Mr. Hamilton's missing daughter, and you are right to suspect him. I am going to speak to the Lakeview police soon. Stay away from him. He's a dangerous man."

He didn't tell her about Laura's ghost. Adults tended not to believe in that stuff. He just thanked her and then decided to call it a night. His head was spinning. Ruthie was acting so erratically, and now they had Joe Hamilton to worry about. Would he really come after them?

As Jalen began to drift off to sleep, a dim light flickered in the corner of his room, pulling him back to awareness. He sat up, eyes wide.

The small glow intensified, morphing into the hazy outline of a teenage girl. She had long hair and an angelic face, clad in pajamas that floated around her like mist. Jalen rubbed his eyes, disbelieving, but when he glanced back, she was still there, translucent enough for him to see his computer desk through her form. His heart raced, and he gripped the sheets tightly.

"Don't be afraid, Jalen," she said. Her voice echoed as if it traveled from a great distance, yet she was mere feet away.

"A-a-are you Laura?" he stammered, battling his fear.

"Yes, I am. I'm not here to hurt you. I want to thank you for what you and your friends have done for Ruthie."

"You're, uh, welcome," he managed, still bewildered.

"She needs you. She doesn't have much time left."

"What do you mean?"

"She's not here for long, Jalen. Her body is failing her. She's come back to seek justice for what was done to her, to make those who ignored her cries for help suffer as she did, and to confront the man who betrayed and murdered her. Ruthie loves you all, but be cautious around her. Try not to upset her. As her body decays, so does her humanity."

"What does that mean?"

"It means Ruthie doesn't want to hurt you, but she's losing control of her mind and body."

"I don't understand." Jalen's confusion deepened. Why would anyone hurt those they didn't want to harm? It made no sense to him.

"I can't find the right words, Jalen. Ruthie was murdered, and now she's risen from the dead seeking justice. Something is controlling her body—something violent—but Ruthie's mind is still there. She recognizes you all. The problem is, as her body decays, so does her mind. She's struggling to remember who she is, why she's here, and for whom. Does that make sense? While the force animating her is beyond our understanding, Ruthie would never hurt you. But as she deteriorates, so does her grip on her anger."

Jalen nodded, trying to grasp the reality, even though uncertainty still lingered.

Laura floated before him, a luminous figure, her long hair drifting around her. He wasn't afraid; he knew he was seeing the ghost of Laura, Joe Hamilton's first daughter.

"What do you mean by the people who 'let her down'?"

"There were adults who could have helped Ruthie—who should have—but they did nothing. They stood by, silent witnesses to her suffering."

Jalen pondered that. How could anyone ignore a little girl in pain? His mother would do anything to protect him; he was certain of that. The thought that some adults wouldn't act was shocking.

"I also need to warn you about Joe," Laura continued. "He knows you have the video footage. He's furious and will come after you if he's not stopped." Jalen felt a chill run through him at her words.

"Ruthie told us. We are all keeping weapons near us and our heads on a swivel. He won't get us," Jalen said this with the bravado of a 12-year-old boy.

"I'm glad. Goodnight Jalen."

"Goodnight, Laura. Thank you."

Laura smiled a sad smile and began to fade before his eyes.

Soon, he could see nothing but his computer desk where she had been.

CHAPTER SIXTEEN

The next morning, Lindsey pulled into the parking lot of the Lakeview Police Station. She had left her home at 4 a.m. so as to arrive early. She gathered up her folder of news articles and research, as well as her courage, and marched in the front door of the station. She just hoped they'd listen to her.

Shortly after, Joe Hamilton arrived at the station. He came in and sat down in the waiting area across from Lindsey. She stared a hole into him from across the room. She hadn't seen him in person since the funeral when she was 14 years old. He looked almost exactly the same, just a little older and with less hair. Her heart was beating fast, but seeing him brought back all the anger she had been feeling through the years since Laura's death.

He finally looked up from his seat where he had been sitting staring at his hands and made eye contact with her. She steeled herself and took a breath to speak when she realized there was no recognition in his eyes. He didn't know who she was.

As she continued to wait, a detective came out to escort Joe to the back.

Before the detective left, he looked at her and said, "Ms. Derringer, someone will be with you shortly."

Joe's eyes widened, and recognition grabbed hold just as the door shut him off from her view. She felt satisfaction knowing that he now knew who she was and likely why she was there.

~ ~ ~

Across town, Jalen slept in. He'd been up late the night before and there'd been a lot for his brain to process.

When he awoke, he immediately hopped onto Discord. He found Pedro and Dakota online. He filled them in on what had happened the night before. At this point, with all that had happened, neither boy was skeptical. He also told them what he found online about the house fire that killed Laura and how he had found Lindsey's website and messaged her.

"I wonder if she's there now?" Dakota asked.

"What do you think Mr. Hamilton will do when he sees her?" Pedro chimed in

"Nothing, dude, they're in a police station," Jalen said.

"I think we're safe as long as we are at home or at the clubhouse, because he doesn't know where it is," Dakota opined.

"I agree with Dakota," Pedro advised.

"Same," Jalen added.

After a brief discussion, the boys decided they would stay inside that day and play video games. They felt certain they were safe in their homes. Plus, they all had their bats and knives. As only children can, they managed to compartmentalize the situation with Ruthie and Joe Hamiton and soon were laughing together and enjoying their game. They played well into the late afternoon.

~ ~ ~

As the day began to give way to night, Ruthie awoke in the treehouse. Once again, her limbs felt heavy and harder to move around. She nibbled on a Pop-Tart and drank a warm Capri-Sun.

Today, she was going to visit her mother.

After finishing her food, Ruthie climbed down the rope ladder and began to make her way to her house. She hadn't been back since the night her stepfather hurt her. It was dusk when her house came into view. She walked across the backyard to the sliding glass door. It was unlocked like it always was.

There was no need to lock the door to keep out danger, the danger lived inside.

She walked past the kitchen table and towards the living room. On the way, she saw her dolly on the floor. The doll's head was smashed, causing her eyes to be askew. She picked up the doll and tucked it lovingly under her arm. Claire was her favorite doll. She had an idea who had smashed her head, and the rage in her began to simmer.

There was no one in the living room, so Ruthie turned and started down the hallway towards her mother's room.

Inside, Julia lay on her bed on her side. Eyes open and staring, but not seeing. She spent most days like that since Ruthie had gone missing.

As she lay there, she heard and saw her doorknob begin to turn. She assumed it was her husband returning home from the police station and rolled over to face the opposite wall.

At that moment, she felt the bed creak, and a small hand touched her shoulder.

Ruthie! Oh my God, it was Ruthie! she thought in a flash and turned quickly to face her daughter.

What she saw took her breath away. It was her daughter kneeling on her bed, or at least she resembled her daughter. Instinctively, Julia grabbed Ruthie and pulled her to her chest, even as her brain was processing what it was seeing. Almost immediately, the sickly-sweet smell of death accosted her, causing her to push Ruthie out to arm's length.

"Mommy, I missed you."

Julia was confused. It was Ruthie's voice, but what it had come out of was the corpse of a little girl, not her Ruthie. Her face was pallid, her cheeks protruded, and her eyes were more sunken than she thought was possible for a living person. Her already tiny frame was wasted away, and her nightdress swallowed her now bony body.

In spite of her doubts, she once again embraced her daughter, and, to her horror, a large piece of skin sloughed off of Ruthie's arm and into her hand.

She looked at the gelatinous strip of skin dangling from her palm and screamed, pushing herself away from her daughter and all the way off the bed until her back was against the wall.

"Mommy, did you miss me too?" the Ruthie creature asked with her almost toothless mouth.

Julia was so confused. She had prayed for this day. She had prayed that Ruthie was safe, unharmed, and would come back to her. What was happening? What was this creature masquerading as her daughter?

"What's wrong, Mommy?" Ruthie cocked her head in a bird-like fashion. The room began to chill.

"Who are you? WHAT are you?" Julia managed to choke out the words as she took in more of Ruthie's appearance.

"Silly mommy. I'm your Ruthie." She broke into a wide gray-gummed smile as a line of drool began to trail down her chin and dangle in the air.

"What's happened to you?" Julia asked, leaning further back from the daughter whose return she had begged God for.

The room chilled further, and Ruthie stopped smiling. She looked down at the floor, clenching her little fists.

It was then that Juia noticed the bald patches of missing hair on Ruthie's head. Then, looking her over, she saw the horrid state of Ruthie's legs. They looked like they had been burned. Strips of flesh were blackened, and others were hanging open in gaping wounds.

Julia screamed again.

This must be a nightmare, she told herself. It has to be.

Ruthie raised her head to face her mother. Her eyes had begun to glow, and the smile was gone from her deteriorating face.

"It IS me, Mommy. Daddy did this to me. He hurt me and left me in the woods."

Julia curled in on herself and put her fisted hands to her mouth.

"NO! No, that's not true!"

"Mommy, why? Why did Daddy hurt me?" Ruthie pleaded with Julia for answers.

"Oh God, no . . . no . . . this isn't happening!" Julia wailed.

Julia began sobbing uncontrollably. Somewhere inside, she had suspected that Joe had hurt her baby. She had turned a blind eye all those years to the abuse to keep the peace in her marriage and the lifestyle to which she had grown accustomed. She did it for both of them, she told herself. Where would they be without Joe? He was the breadwinner in the family and yes, he had a heavy hand, but kill her? She couldn't accept it.

"Answer me, Mommy! DADDY HURT ME! WHY DIDN'T YOU SAVE ME?"

Ruthie's voice got louder as an unseen wind began to tear through the room, throwing papers up into the air and blowing her hair wildly around her face. Her eyes glowed bright, and her fists were again balled at her sides.

Julia closed her eyes to the sight and slid down the wall to the floor. Ruthie crawled across the bed towards her and slipped off the bed and down onto the floor with her. The wind stopped and the glow in her eyes extinguished.

"Mommy, please."

Ruthie's voice was quiet and pleading. Brown tears began to leak from her eyes and make their way down her ruined little face. Julia opened her eyes to see her Ruthie's once sparkling blue eyes staring into hers intently. She pulled her into her arms and squeezed her tightly.

"I'm sorry, baby. I'm so very sorry. Oh God, what have I done? My baby! My poor sweet baby!" Julia sobbed and rocked with Ruthie tight against her chest. Whatever this was, hallucination or not, she knew now for sure that her daughter was dead.

She was dead, and he killed her.

Just then, the bedroom door flew open. It was Joe!

"What the hell is going on in here? I heard scream—" he was beginning to say when his eyes landed on the scene before him. His wife, on the floor of their bedroom between the bed and the wall, clutching what could only be the corpse of Ruthie.

How was that possible? He had buried her. He went deep into the woods. There was no way Julia could have found her. Then, the corpse turned her head and looked at him. Her eyes were glowing. Her head balding and her skin decomposing, it was a horrifying sight. Anyone else would have been terrified, but Joe Hamilton felt nothing but rage. The girl could never do as she was told! Even in death, she couldn't stay still and obey him!

He launched himself across the bed and ripped Ruthie from Julia's arms.

He grabbed her by the shoulders and began to pound her head against the wall screaming, "Why-can't-you-just-stay-dead?!"

He had caught Ruthie off guard. The preternatural strength that had inhabited her body before seemed as if it was used up, and she was unable to free herself from his hands as he smashed her head against the wall. Her head began to soften on the back as he forcefully slammed it against the wall, causing it to become misshapen.

Ruthie struggled to summon the rage that had carried her this far, but it seemed, even in death, he could overpower Ruthie. Her strength was failing her. She clawed at his face and tried to wriggle out of his grasp, but it was no use.

Suddenly, there was a loud CRACK! When Ruthie looked up, she saw her mother standing over them both holding a lamp. She had hit him as hard as she could over the head. Blood began to pour from the wound, and Joe Hamilton moaned.

"RUN! RUN RUTHIE!" her mother screamed at her.

Ruthie struggled to her feet and made her way to the doorway, almost dragging her burned leg. She glanced back one more time at her mother and saw her mouth the words, "I love you" and then "I'm sorry" before she raised the lamp again.

Ruthie stumbled out of the house and into the woods. She just needed to make it to the clubhouse, but her limbs were failing her, and her vision was askew from her broken skull.

A light appeared in front of her. It was Laura.

"Come on, Ruthie. Come towards me. You can do this. You can make it."

Ruthie moved towards Laura's light, struggling and limping as her body's movements became harder and harder to control. After what seemed like forever, she collapsed at the foot of the treehouse. Ruthie felt herself floating in the air as Laura lifted her and then deposited on the sleeping bags in the clubhouse. She had made it, but he had beaten her again, and she lay down on the sleeping bags, unable to rise.

CHAPTER SEVENTEEN

Jalen and the boys were still playing video games when Laura's light burst into Jalen's room. The light fluttered around furiously in front of Jalen, not yet forming into Laura's shape.

"Guys! Laura is here!"

"What?" Pedro exclaimed.

"The ghost is there now?" Dakota asked excitedly.

"Yeah, she's flying around my room like crazy."

The light was furiously flying around the room, knocking action figures off the shelves and throwing up paper.

"What's going on, Laura?"

Jalen didn't understand why she was throwing things around his room and began to become afraid. He stood up from the floor, and the light stopped right in front of him. Within the light was Laura's panicked face. She was moving her mouth furiously, but he couldn't hear her at all.

"She's trying to say something, but she can't seem to talk now." He relayed the scene to the other boys. "Her mouth is moving, but nothing is coming out."

As if frustrated with the situation, the light blew through the closet doors and flung them open from the inside, sending his clothes flying all over the room. Jalen began to back up towards his bedroom door. He had never seen anything like this, and he was becoming more afraid, even though Laura told him she would never hurt him.

Finally, the glowing ball stopped moving and then slowly floated in front of Jalen. He could make out Laura's face and could see panic and anguish in her expression. She was trying to calm herself, he realized.

"Okay, deep breath, Laura. What are you trying to tell me? Is Joe on his way?"

She shook her head no, seemed to close her eyes and try to calm herself. When her eyes re-opened, she looked deep into Jalen's eyes and willed a message to him as hard as she could.

Jalen began to hear her voice in his head.

"Ruthie . . . Joe . . . hurt her . . . treehouse . . ."

Those were the only words he could make out, but they were enough. Joe had somehow found Ruthie and hurt her. Jalen told Pedro and Dakota to meet him at the park, that it was an emergency, and to bring their weapons.

Dakota immediately tip-toed up the stairs to see if his mothers were in the living room. They weren't there, and he could hear their television playing from inside their bedroom. He went back to the kitchen, opened a drawer, and grabbed a large knife. He felt like this situation would likely call for more than his pocket knife. He shoved it into his backpack and headed back downstairs.

He quietly opened the newly repaired sliding glass door and slipped out.

Jalen's mom wasn't home, but she had left a babysitter there for the girls. He opened his bedroom window and jumped out onto the roof of their porch. From there, he ran to the tree growing near the side of the porch and climbed down.

Pedro's parents were working late, so he was able to grab his bat, grab his backpack, and dash out the door. He was filled with anxiety as he ran the three blocks to the park entrance, worrying about what had happened to Ruthie. He knew he should have gone to check on her instead of playing video games all day.

The three boys met at the entrance of the park. All three arrived at almost the same time, Dakota was the last to arrive as he lived a couple blocks further away than the other two.

"What's going on?" Pedro immediately asked Jalen.

"I don't know. I told you all I know. We need to get to the clubhouse now."

Dakota pulled a flashlight out of his bag, and Jalen stopped him before he turned it on.

"No flashlights. What if Mr. Hamilton is in the woods?"

The thought of Mr. Hamilton being somewhere out in the woods made a pit form in Pedro's stomach. The boys had been to the clubhouse enough times to get there in the dark, it was just less scary with a flashlight.

The boys moved quietly through the trees. Their path was lit only by the moonlight. It was late, and at any point any one of the boys' parents could discover they were gone, but they weren't worried about the consequences of sneaking out. They were solely focused on Ruthie.

A bird flew up out of a bush and made all three of the boys jump. They continued on their way, trying not to snap twigs or kick pine needles as they approached. They passed Ruthie's grave, and a collective chill ran through their spines.

~ ~ ~

As the boys made their way through the quiet forest, another figure moved in the dark, unseen, headed to make sure Ruthie was in her grave where she belonged.

Julia lay unconscious, maybe dead, back at the house. Joe had gone into a blind rage when he came to from the blow on the head she had delivered. He beat her until she couldn't stand any longer and made not even a gurgle out of her blood-filled mouth.

Even if she hadn't attacked him, she had to go. She knew his secret and kept screaming at him about killing "her baby." Now, Joe needed to make sure that Ruthie was in her grave and then decide how to deal with the other loose ends.

He had seen that interfering bitch, Lindsey, at the police station today. No doubt there to dredge up his past and Laura. It had taken all his control not to attack her there and then. He knew he should have handled her before he left town, but he hadn't wanted to risk it at the time.

~ ~ ~

The clubhouse came into sight. The battery-operated lights Pedro had strung inside for Ruthie glowed eerily in the dark. There were no sounds from the clubhouse. The boys ran the rest of the way there and one by one climbed the rope and went inside.

Ruthie lay bundled in her sleeping bags, not moving.

Pedro got to her first and was taken aback by her appearance. Her head was misshapen and grotesque to look at. Jalen and Dakota were right behind him.

"Ruthie, who did this?" Jalen asked her.

Pedro's eyes had filled with tears, and Dakota had turned away, nauseated by the sight of her little head.

"Mommy . . . Mommy saved me," was all she managed to get out before she fell back into unconsciousness.

"What are we going to do now?" Jalen turned to the other two boys, wide-eyed. This was too much. How were they supposed to know what to do? He felt panic beginning to rise up within himself.

"I don't know. Look at her! Look at her head! Oh my God!" is all that Pedro could say.

"We have to make a decision. We have to do something. We can't just leave her here." Jalen said, looking from Pedro to Dakota.

The boys' anxiety was palpable. The three 12-year-old boys now wished there was an adult with them.

Pedro moved back over to the very still little girl lying on the sleeping bags and gently placed his hand over hers. He was openly crying now.

"Well, well, well . . . what would your parents say if they knew you were out here in the woods so late at night?"

All three boys spun around to see Joe Hamilton standing in their clubhouse. The moonlight shone on his contorted face. It was the face of a madman.

Pedro sprang into action and barreled towards Joe with his bat. He swung at him, full of righteous anger, and connected with Joe's shoulder.

The blow knocked him back a step, but Joe quickly recovered his balance, rolled his shoulder a bit, and said, "Is that all you've got?"

Faster than Pedro could duck, he backhanded Pedro with all his strength, catching Pedro in the head. His body flew backwards and landed near the pile of sleeping bags containing tiny Ruthie. He moaned but didn't get up.

The other two boys had run to the other side of the clubhouse and armed themselves with their knives, Jalen with a pocket knife and Dakota with the large kitchen knife.

"Boys, boys, boys . . . there's no need for all this. Just put down the knives, and I'll take Ruthie and leave. Then, we can all leave this treehouse alive," he said darkly, as his flat, soulless eyes told them otherwise.

"Fuck you! You're not getting her!" Jalen yelled. He held the knife in front of him, hand shaking.

"Yeah, fuck you, dude," Dakota added and raised his knife as he stood beside Jalen.

"Language boys! What do I tell you all about using foul language? Intelligent young men do not need to resort to cursing. Tsk, tsk."

"Okay, well in that case, DOUBLE FUCK YOU!" yelled Dakota as he sprang towards him, knife in hand.

Joe snatched the knife from Dakota and sliced him across the cheek. The cut immediately welled up with blood and started to bleed. Dakota stood there, too shocked to move as Joe raised the knife once again and brought it down with all the force a madman has. Dakota's eyes widened as the blade came towards him. But before it made contact, Joe's arm was knocked down hard, and the knife clattered to the floor.

Pedro was back up and swinging for the fences. He followed up the first hit with another to the back of Joe's legs, causing him to drop to his knees.

Pedro then dashed towards the other boys, but Joe was quicker. He grabbed Pedro's leg and pulled him down to the ground.

That's when Jalen attacked, stabbing wildly into Joe's shoulder with his pocket knife.

With one hand holding Pedro down, Joe used the other to grab Jalen's wrist and wrench the knife free, breaking Jalen's wrist in the process.

"Ahhh!!" Jalen screamed and fell to his knees cradling his broken wrist.

Joe got to his feet, towering over the three wounded boys.

"I don't have time for this shit. It's over boys," Joe snarled.

He reached around behind him and picked up the baseball bat.

Pedro ran to Jalen's side, and Dakota went to his other side. They grabbed Jalen, and all three boys got to their feet, still willing to fight this full-grown man to save Ruthie.

Joe began to ferociously swing the bat, knocking all three boys down. Pedro's nose was bleeding. It just added to the pool of blood on the floor from Dakota's cut.

He caught Jalen in his broken arm, who went pale as a ghost, then to the floor.

Another swing caught Dakota in his back, and he yelped in pain.

Joe laughed loudly as he swung. The boys were backed up to the wall. This was it. Pedro covered Jalen with his body, and Dakota did the same. They tensed for the blow

Joe raised the bat one more time, feinting blows to torture the boys with their impending deaths.

"What made you think you could stop me? You puny little shits," he taunted them.

Then, the air suddenly chilled, and the wind picked up. Pedro chanced a glance up and saw two glowing orbs in the dark behind Joe.

Ruthie.

She moved like a cat, swift and with purpose. She ran towards her father, grabbing the clubhouse rope on her way. She leaped onto his back, screaming and wrapping the rope around Joe's neck. Around and around, she wrapped it. Joe began trying to hit her with the bat to get him off his back. He landed two blows, but Ruthie kept going.

He fought desperately to free himself from her grip. The wounded boys could only watch helplessly.

He grabbed handfuls of her hair and ripped them out. The blonde hair drifted through the air like down from a blanket. He then tried to wrench her hands free of the rope as his face turned red from the rope.

"Little . . . ergh . . . bitch," he managed to strangle out of his mouth. "Why . . . didn't . . . you . . . stay . . . dead?!" he gasped.

The struggle seemed to go on forever, and Ruthie was making little progress in her bid to stop him. He was struggling to breathe, but still upright, and it seemed she was losing steam. Then, he managed to pry one of her tiny hands off the rope around his neck and fling her to the floor. She did not get up.

He straightened himself up and began to unwrap the rope from his neck when, out of nowhere, a force shoved him. He lost his balance and pinwheeled his arms trying to get it back, but it was too late. He was too close to the hole in the floor.

Once he fell, he went straight down, hungry gravity grabbing at him. The rope jerked tight, and he kicked his feet trying to touch the ground. With his eyes bulging from his head and spittle flying from his lips, he kicked twice, three times, then stopped.

Joe Hamilton was dead. His body swung slowly from side to side on the rope in the moonlight.

Julia stood up and rushed immediately to her daughter while the boys struggled to their feet and joined her. She was badly beaten herself and didn't know how she was even conscious. She had managed to drag herself off the floor and go after Joe when he left the house. She was determined to keep him from Ruthie. When she arrived at the clubhouse, she spotted the rope ladder hanging down the back side of the structure. Slowly and painfully, she had made her way up.

Ruthie looked at her mother and smiled a toothless, precious smile. Her face was haggard and tired. The boys gathered around her, bleeding and broken, but still alive.

"It's time, Mommy. You have to put me back."

Julia began to sob and pulled her daughter, the one she had failed so miserably, to her in a tight embrace.

"What does she mean? Put her back?" Jalen asked, looking at Julia.

A ball of light floated up over Joe's body, seeming to pause at his face and then into the treehouse. Soon, the translucent image of Laura stood before them, beaming.

"She did it. Ruthie fulfilled her duty to herself, to me, and to every child that man ever hurt. That means her time here on earth is done."

"NO!" Julia squeezed Ruthie tighter.

"Julia, you have to place her back in her grave. Her soul needs to rest, and, more practically, the police need to find her so that you can place her in an even better place to rest. Let me help."

Laura floated to Ruthie's side and took her from Julia's arms gently. Ruthie smiled at her.

Light filled the clubhouse, and they saw Ruthie's body begin to float across the clubhouse and out of the window. The boys and Julia hurried as fast as they could to get out of the clubhouse's back entrance, down a rope ladder that hung off the back.

It was slow going as they were all injured and bloodied. Julia winced as she climbed down from her broken ribs and bruised arms. Her face was a bloody mess. The boys looked no better.

By the time they all helped each other down, Laura had reached the gravesite, and Ruthie was slowly pulling dirt over her legs. When they arrived, she spoke in her hoarse voice and told them they needed to finish it.

"I have to be covered back up."

Her mother nodded that she understood, wiped away tears, and began to push the dirt over her only child.

The boys fell to their knees and helped to move dirt onto her body, Jalen using his good arm. No words were spoken, but all four were crying. This was it. Ruthie was going for good. She had done what she came here to do, and now her time was up.

Laura hovered nearby, lighting their workspace until they had covered all of Ruthie except her tiny face.

"Thank you, Pedro, Jalen, and Dakota. I love you. You are the best big brothers anyone could ever have."

"We love you too, Ruthie," Pedro managed to choke out in between sobs.

"We'll miss you," Jalen said, his face full of anguish.

"Don't cry. I won't be too far away." Ruthie smiled.

"Wait!" Dakota turned and ran back to the clubhouse. A couple minutes later he emerged from the dark carrying Ruthie's doll and placed it in the grave beside her.

"Thank you, Dakota."

The boys stepped back from the grave to give her mother some space with Ruthie. Julia leaned in and kissed Ruthie on the forehead.

"I love you, my sweet girl. I'm so sorry I let you down."

"I forgive you, Mommy."

And with that Ruthie closed her eyes forever.

EPILOGUE

The boys huddled together next to Ruthie's grave. Injured and exhausted, they didn't know what to do with themselves.

Julia dragged herself to her feet and walked over to check on them. Once she was satisfied that they could walk, she told them to go home the back way. As they were leaving, they heard the sound of hound dogs baying.

The police found Julia sitting down propped up against a tree near Ruthie's grave, bloodied and weak. She explained that she had figured out that Joe had killed Ruthie, and a confrontation ensued. He had admitted it to her and told her where he buried the body. Then attempted to beat her to death. After that, he left, thinking she was dead, to go move Ruthie's body. She wasn't going to allow that. Because of her injuries, her progress was slow, and by the time she reached Ruthie's grave, Joe was nowhere to be seen. She heard a commotion from up ahead, and when she went to investigate, she found Joe hanging from the treehouse by his neck. He was dead.

After the visit from Lindsey, the police had placed Joe under surveillance. Once the surveillance team got word back to the station that Joe was on the move, they got their team together to follow where he had gone in hopes of finding Ruthie's body. Joe did them one better. He led them to two bodies: Ruthie's and his own.

Julia chose to leave the boys out of it. They had been through enough, and their presence would have only caused more questions.

The boys spent the rest of their summer grounded by their parents for sneaking out and taking their bikes to the bike trail, where they got their injuries after tumbling down the mountain trail. Although their parents were skeptical of their story, the boys stuck to it and, in the end, they had no choice but to accept it.

Jalen had a cast on his wrist all summer, and Dakota had a cool scar. Pedro was sore and bruised with a bump on his head, but otherwise okay.

The police announced that Ruthie was dead, and her case had been solved. Her funeral was held the next week. Hundreds of people attended.

Soon after, Julia moved back to her hometown in Florida.

The boys never returned to the clubhouse.

ACKNOWLEDGMENTS

To my wonderful Alpha Readers:

I could never have done this without your support, understanding, and love. Thank you.

Stacey Humberson Prado

Jim Gibson (Dad)

To my outstanding BETA readers!!

THANK YOU for your time and dedication to helping me get this book out into the world. Your help was invaluable.

Jim Riley

Olivia Meek

Sandy Perez

Cindy Martin

Michele Blair

Angie Teske

Bonnie Scherr

ABOUT THE AUTHOR

Angie Gibson lives in Northwest Georgia with her son, a dog named Stella, and two furry familiars named Hemingway and The Tookus.

She likes to spend time with family, reading, watching true crime shows, thrift shop hunting, and dabbling in different kinds of art mediums.

Angie works a full-time job during the day and is a writer by night. She believes in UFOs, ghosts, Sasquatches, and lots of cryptids. Therefore, her mind is always swirling with ideas for books. She spends much of her time chasing those ideas around and trying to land them on pages.

Made in the USA
Middletown, DE
28 February 2025

72012186R00108